THOSE WHO ARE GONE

a novelette

Lawrence F. Lihosit

© Copyright 2022, Lawrence F. Lihosit All rights reserved.

FIRST EDITION
October, 2022

All rights reserved. No part of this book may be used or reproduced by any means, graphic, electronic, or mechanical, including photocopying, recording, taping or by any information storage retrieval system without the written permission of the author except in the case of brief quotations embodied in critical articles and reviews.

Printed by KDP, an Amazon.com company, the printing location may vary, depending upon where the book is to be delivered since this is a Print-On-Demand book.

front cover watercolor: Tim Bhajjan©
interior ink sketch: the author
Cover Consultant: Daniel Gonzalez
Editors: Will James & Bryant Wieneke
Copy Readers: Larry Latimer,
Anson, Maggie & Zeke Lihosit

ISBN 9798352366608
Fiction
Historical Novelette

P R I N T E D   I N   T H E   U. S. A.

For the Thunderbirds, class of 1964-1965

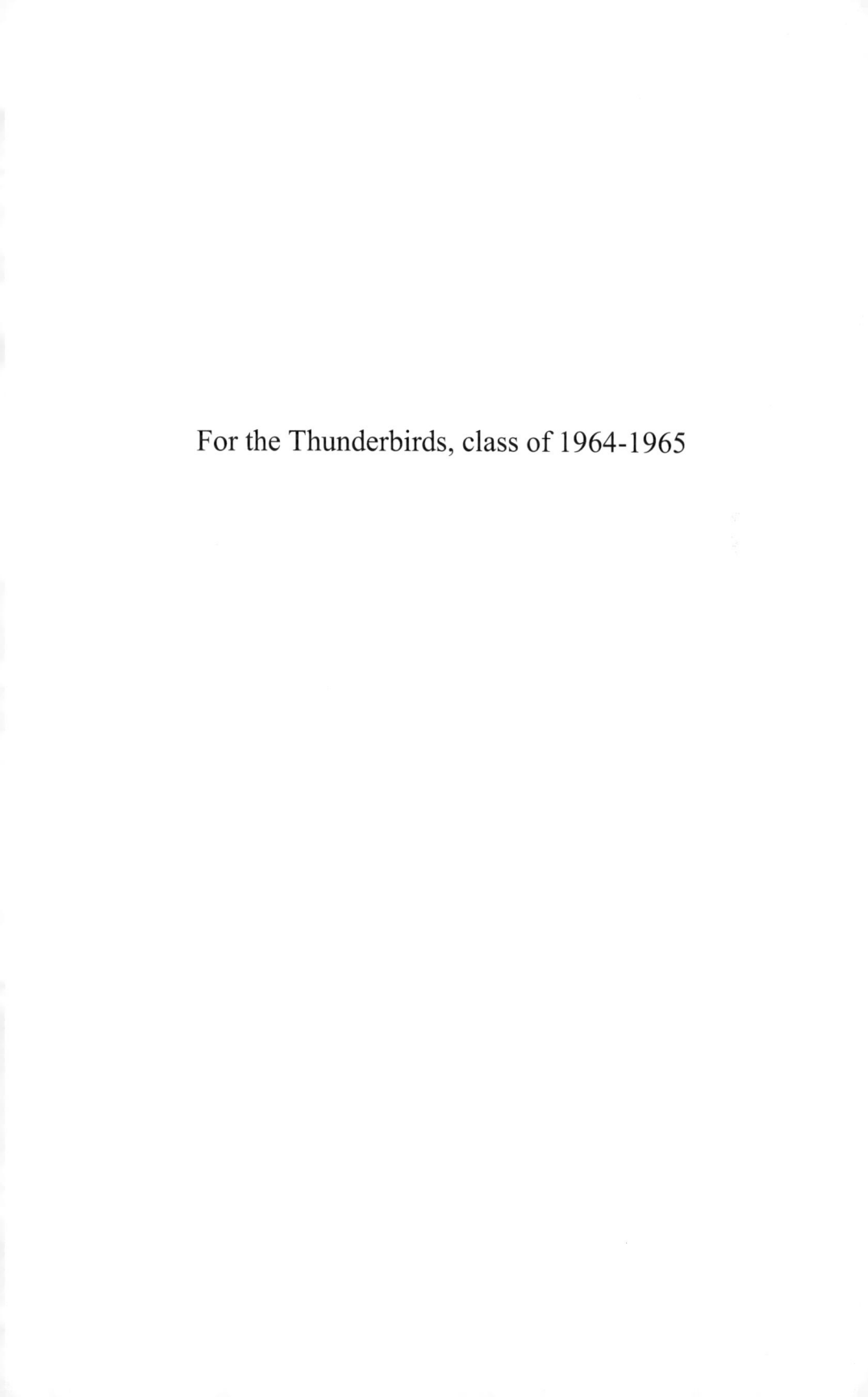

Those Who Are Gone

We all began to sprout coarse, dark, curly hairs here and there. Our voices cracked and then went down an octave. We noticed girls. The television news covered a story about three armed ships off the coast of Vietnam which opened fire on an American battleship and were sunk. Congress voted to let the President do whatever was necessary. Our lives were about to change and everything was like that first dust devil I ever saw down by the *arroyo* which ran north to south, just a few blocks from our home.

That's where I met him, in the wash, only days after arriving while exploring the new neighborhood on my bicycle during the early morning hours when small birds chirped in the mesquite trees on either side of the creek.

I pedaled down a dry, dusty path. The wash might have been twenty feet lower than 76th Street and even lower than our school, built on fill. It was a gentle slope. The bottom was mostly flat, with some sediment deposits from the last flood, a few small mounds from dumped fill and sage brush. There was a screen of mesquite along the creek. As I wound around the fill, I heard voices in Spanish. Nobody in my neighborhood back east spoke Spanish.

There was a group of boys about my age setting a large plywood panel on a small mound of dirt, a ramp. Just a hundred yards away, pieces of dried sage brush lifted into the air with orange clay dust and swirled. It grew in microseconds like a giant, brown, semitransparent monster, one hundred feet in the air, swirling faster and faster. We all stood without speaking. I had seen tornados back east but never this close. The brown funnel became huge and zig-zagged randomly. As quickly as it had formed, it just stopped swirling and the dry sticks and dust fell.

I approached the boys. "What was that?"

The boys started laughing and made some remarks in Spanish. One boy walked over and stuck out his hand, to shake. "It was a dust devil. You must not be from around here. I'm Vic Chacón." While we talked, the other boys started to take turns racing up the ramp and for a brief second, they were airborne. Then, they all rode over around me. Vic introduced us. "This is Jesus Monguilla, called Chucho, Anastasio Cuca, called Tacho, Jose Maria Leyca, called Cájame and Luis de Silva, called Wuicho. *Muchachos,* this is Jack Colter."

We spent almost an hour taking turns jumping the ramp. We started doing tricks. Chucho let go of his handlebars while in flight. Cájame crossed his arms while in flight. Vic did a back flip. Then a tall boy with blond hair pulled up.

"Chief! Mind if I take a jump?"

No one spoke. Cájame and Wuicho tied a length of rope onto the plywood, attached it to Tacho's bike and they pedaled away towards the creek. "Beaners! Go back to Mexico!" yelled the tall boy.

Vic waved for me to follow. We stopped at a rickety four-foot wide, unpainted wooden bridge. The creek was several feet lower and shaded. The water gurgled. Chucho and Tacho untied the ramp and laid it under mesquite and *palo verde*. "That was Eric Wetzel, a jerk — *un jalado*," said Vic.

"*Muy jalado*," said Wuicho and everyone laughed.

"*Eh la moey*," said Chucho and everyone laughed again.

"So, if *jalado* is a jerk, what is '*Eh la moey*'?" I asked.

"It's like 'cool'," responded Vic. "Come to my house. My grandmother will have something good to drink."

Yaqui Town only had vehicular access to the north onto McDowell Road via a paved alley between a used car lot and a liquor store. We entered from the south along a clay path which led to a narrow gravel street with make-shift street lights that nightly threw lopsided beams across the neighborhood, built on the downslope alongside the wash. As we pedaled down the road, dogs barked. A large mutt chased Chucho who called to the dog, "*Cálmate*," but the dog snapped. Chucho threw a rock and the dog stopped.

The lots were irregular, like shards of broken glass, divided by Mexican fence post cactus and chicken wire nailed to crude wooden posts. In between the posts were dried mesquite sticks. The houses were all different sizes and construction. The southern-most homes were windowless and smaller, some made of lashed sticks covered with mud. They had metal water towers. Others had windows and wooden siding. Some had peaked roofs and others had flat roofs. No one had manicured lawns but many had gardens and almost all had religious articles like statues or pictures on wooden posts with candles underneath.

Vic lived on the northmost irregular lot in a house that cantilevered off the slope near the creek. The house had unpainted picket fencing on the street side with a stretch of fence post cactus on part of the side and chicken wire around the rest of the side and back where his family had a small garden. The creek brush line screened it from the other side, about a quarter mile away. Vic carefully lifted the wire latch and we all pushed our bikes through, parked them on the side of the house where they had leveled an outdoor meeting area: a picnic table covered by a simple shade structure made of dried mesquite wood lashed together.

Soon, Vic followed his grandmother out the front door. carrying plastic glasses in one hand and a pitcher of a red drink. As the old woman with a long single grey braid which hung halfway down the back of her cotton print dress took the glasses individually to place them before us. The boys all greeted her.

"*Buenos días, Doña Romualda.*"

"*Buenos días, distinguidos. Espero qué les guste el agua de tamarindo.*"

She began to pour each of us a glass. I turned to Vic and whispered, "What did she say?"

Vic said, "This is *tamarindo* juice mixed with water. It's sweet." Then he told his grandmother that I didn't speak Spanish.

"*Bienvenido, fuego,*" she said. Then turning to everyone she said, "*Juntos van a triunfar.*" Romualda smiled wide showing some amazingly white teeth, a few with gold fillings around the edges like braces.

Vic translated. "She called you red head and said that together we would triumph." Everyone smiled and we lifted our plastic glasses. "Triumph."

Only a short time later, there was a knock on our front door which is how I met Jed Smith who wondered if my parents might like their gaslight cleaned. My mom was busy putting a stinky purple colored solution on her hair to bleach it blond. "Go in my purse and get a few dollars out. If I leave this on too long, my hair will fall out," she said.

I went out to talk while Jed worked. The same age as me, he lived up the street and would also enter the eighth grade. Jed unfolded his three-step ladder and carefully laid out all of his tools on the sidewalk.

"Have you lived here long?" I asked.

"About a year," he answered as he put on thick gloves.

"Where did you come from?"

"Colorado. My dad works for Weyerhaeuser and he was involved with logging. They offered him an eight to five job managing a lumberyard."

He knew Vic, so I invited him to jump the ramps. The next morning, we rode towards Yavapai School and Jed stopped at a house just up the street from school where another future peer lived — Jim Bridger. His parents had moved to Scottsdale from Missouri two years before. He unlocked a tool shed and pulled his bicycle out as we talked. Jim had a fresh haircut and it was oiled and combed perfectly. While Jed and I wore cut-off blue jeans and worn t-shirts, Jim wore stylish Bermuda shorts and a fancy golf shirt. Golf was as much a mystery to me as the Gulf of Mexico. We mounted our bicycles and Jim explained how his family dated back to Plymouth Rock and his dad was a bank manager. "And what about your family?" he asked me.

"I don't know much about them. According to my mom, our ancestors came from Central Europe and immigrated as laborers. My dad explained that we made things work."

We were joined by Chris Carson who knew both Jim and Jed. His father, a Second World War fighter pilot, now an architect. They had moved to Scottsdale months before from a job at Travis Airforce Base, California where his dad had designed and supervised the construction of hundreds of new housing units.

Like Jed and me, he didn't know much about his family tree. "My dad says that the way things are hopping at Williams and Luke Air Force Bases, we'll be here a while," he told us.

He sported worn clothing and didn't get a haircut once a month. Jed had two sisters and an older brother. Chris had an older brother like me. Jim was an only child.

Now we had quite a crew with our early mornings filled with laughter and sometimes jeers. They were also filled with our first Spanish lessons. After learning curse words, we moved on to simple sentences.

"How do you say 'I'm thirsty'"

"*Tengo sed.*"

"How do you say, 'Let's go to Skaggs Drugs for an ice cream'."

"*Vamos a Skaggs por un helado.*"

"Maybe it's easier to say *'Vamos a Skaggs'.*"

We started exploring the town. We pedaled north to Osborn where Vic showed us the area where he and his family had lived before buying a lot in Yaqui Town. It was cheap labor housing specifically for Yaqui Indians who had been recruited to work on the Valley of Sun's canals.

"My dad told me that they tried recruiting all sorts of people but settled on the Yaquis who knew canals and farming from Mexico. More importantly, they worked hard and were known as 'Mexico's working men,'" explained Vic.

Chucho and Tacho's families had also lived in the Osborn labor housing while Wuicho and Cájame's families had lived in Guadalupe, a few miles south, the largest Yaqui settlement north of Tucson.

As we sat looking at the old dilapidated labor housing, Cájame said, "There was no border patrol until 1924. People just walked freely back and forth."

"Didn't the American government require them to learn English?" asked Jim.

"Why?" asked Cájame.

"Well, it's our national language," said Jim.

"I read that the Continental Congress had a committee vote on a national language. When German lost by one vote, they tabled it. It's still tabled. There is no national language," deadpanned Cájame. "How many do you speak, Jim?

"Well, one. Everyone speaks English."

Vic glanced at the group. Wuicho said, "*Eh la moey*" and laughed.

"So, you speak English and Spanish, right?" asked Jim

"And Yaqui," replied Vic. "*Yanti jote' ewame-peace,* dude."

As the summer progressed, our early morning bike trips became longer and we even began to pack snacks. Ten of us, five from each side of the creek, pedaled west to the Arizona Canal where we detoured along a canal maintenance road. Once a hundred yards from McDowell Road, we could hear the bushes rustle just before birds took to flight. There were crackling noises when critters ran. We pedaled up to the backside of Papago Park where we could get onto the park's paved roads that curly-cued around artificial lakes and on to Hole in the Rock. We approached it from the north which was a steep, even slope rising about 200 feet, pedaling as long as we could before dropping our bicycles and running. It was early and the park was closed.

The red butte had a windblown hole eroded through it near the top. We climbed up the last rise to the hole big enough for several people to walk through at once. On each side of the hole were flat areas with a view north to Scottsdale and a view south to Tempe. A gentle wind made a low whistling noise as it passed through. It felt like a fan.

We each had a brown bag lunch but agreed to swap. I ended up with aluminum foil wrapped something and two green *chiles* in exchange for a peanut butter and grape jelly on doughy, bleached-white bread.

"It's a *burrito* with meat, beans and rice," said Wuicho. "The *chiles* are pickled. Can I have one?" Once I nodded he grabbed one and explained, "Bite with your front teeth and move it back to the back of your tongue before swallowing. Then, take a bite of the *burrito*."

I didn't follow directions and bit into the *chile* with my molars. My mouth tingled hot and it must have made my face red because the boys all laughed and one handed me a canteen. "It burns more on the way out," said Cájame and everyone laughed again.

"My dad had a Gringo friend at work and they traded food too. The friend burned his tongue so they bought an ice cream cone. Later, in the bathroom, my dad heard the Gringo shout, 'Come on ice cream!'" There was more laughter.

The meat in the *burrito* had a pungent taste that didn't wash away with water. Vic explained that it was javelina. "My dad went hunting."

We stayed at the Hole in the Rock for a good while, enjoying the funneled breeze until the temperatures began to rise. We stuffed our paper garbage and canteen into our backpacks and someone took off running down the towards the bikes as he yelled, "Last one down is a *pendejo*"

We all started running. Overweight, I was last. It was steep and soon, my legs were moving faster than I could keep up with. I took a superman dive, sliding along gravel, arms extended. Both of my arms got chewed up and bled. As I got up, the group came back. Vic immediately took off his t-shirt and ripped off two long strips, telling Chucho to rinse my forearms with canteen water. Then, he wrapped each arm and tied off the bandages.

We rode off but the arms were bleeding through the rags. "Let's head for my house. Romualda can help us."

Romualda motioned me over to a plain wooden table covered by a blue plastic covering. She unwrapped the arms and ordered Vic and his younger sister to grab things for her as she carefully inspected the wounds. Soon, she dabbed them clean and then with a sharp knife, she fileted some long, fat leaves to expose a yellowish flesh inside.

"*Sabila,*" muttered Romualda as she laid the cool, neatly cut and flattened fleshy leaves on my arms before wrapping them up with cotton gauze. Turning to Vic, she gave instructions in Spanish which he translated.

Lawrence F. Lihosit

"Romualda says that your mother should change the dressing twice a day for a day or two. She'll give you some more leaves. Put them in the refrigerator."

Turf Paradise, the race horse track where my dad took the winning circle photos, was closed in the summer. He made some money as a photo journalist for the local newspapers, magazines and the police, taking photos as evidence. That day, he was a bit late for dinner. My mom had food on the table when he opened the door. "Hello. Hello. Long day taking photos of corpses," he said as he walked to the kitchen where he washed his hands at the sink.

"That won't be in the papers," said my mom.

"Nope. Evidence in someone's file. Where's Dan?"

"He's at Canyon Lake."

When my dad sat down, he noticed my bandaged arm. "What happened?"

"Bike spill."

"Does it hurt?" he asked as he swished mashed potatoes on his plate.

"Not now."

"Let's check it out at the hospital after dinner. You know, today's work reminded me of that old murder mystery. They couldn't afford a corpse so they filmed a slight injury mystery and called it Anatomy of a Sprained Ankle."

Later, a nurse diligently unwrapped my forearms. He pulled over a giant magnifying glass on wheels, snapped on a light and studied. "Nice and clean. No sign of infection. Someone did a good job."

"Have you ever heard of *sabila*?" I asked.

"Sure. Aloevera. It's magical."

When I told him about Vic's grandma, he smiled. "A Yaqui *curandera*. They know their stuff."

"Aren't they witches?" asked my dad.

"All medicines come from plants and they have thousands of years experimenting with plants. Did she have horns?"

I laughed. "No."

"There you go. Our Yaqui community can't afford hospitals and generally take care of themselves with the help of their *curanderas* They're not the only ones. A burn specialist here spent four years in the Bolivian Andes where the Aymara people have their own shamans, renowned for thousands of years. One day while walking along a mountain path, a Bolivian friend of his passed quickly, weeping as he carried his burned six-year-old son. The doctor chased him down, offering to help. The man explained as he jogged that the boy had been struck by lightning and in their culture, the only one who could save him would be another person who had also been struck and survived.

The man took off again, the doctor running behind. The man shouted as he approached a wooden two room hut and the door opened. A white haired man dressed in rags spoke to the doctor's Bolivian friend in Aymara, not Spanish, so my doctor didn't understand.

The old man dressed in rags took the boy and immediately carried him into the back room, closing the door. Our doctor and his Bolivian friend sat down on simple, unfinished wooden chairs at a wooden table and waited. They heard Aymara phrases, a rattle, a whistle, then a flute.

The Bolivian explained to our doctor that the old man had also been struck by lightning as a boy and survived with the help of his local *kallawaya*- a *curandero*. In payment, the boy became his apprentice.

That night, the two men had fallen asleep, hunched over the simple table and were awoken by the door opening.

The old man came out, closed the door and asked them to stand. He took dried roots from shelves on his walls, cut them and then pulverized them with a mortar and pestle. He added powders and a bit of water stored in a clay jar. He carefully placed a salve on a plate and went back into the room, closing the door behind him. The sounds of flutes, whistles and rattle continued.

Four days passed, the *kallawaya* only leaving the boy to eat and relieve himself. Finally on the fifth morning, the *kallawaya* opened the door and motioned that the two men could enter. They found the child playing on the floor with a rattle. The doctor told me that the boy had third degree burns on forty percent of his body. Yet, the wounds had all closed over.

The doctor told me that even in Scottsdale's burn unit, after extensive skin grafts and massive doses of antibiotics, the boy would have died.'

The moral of this story is that even if we do not understand something, it does not make it bad. Maybe what we lack today is a bit of simple respect. So what did your *curandera* recommend?"

"She told me to put more *sabila* on twice a day for two days."

"Good. Follow her orders. If the skin turns white or swells, come back."

"Don't you want to inject him with some antibiotics?" asked my dad.

"If it ain't broke don't fix it," said the nurse as he pulled off a rubber glove.

In the parking lot, my dad turned the key to start the car. "Here's some money," he said as he handed me ten dollars. "Tomorrow, ride your bike to Papago Plaza and buy a bouquet for Vic's granny."

I called Vic and arranged for him to translate. The next day, Vic and I knocked on Romualda's door which was next to Vic's house.

"*Buenos dias, fuego,*" she said and smiled.

I handed her the flowers and thanked her for tending my arms which Vic translated. She sat us down at a small table covered with a flowered plastic table cloth. Bowls, spoons and plastic glasses were already set, glasses upside down.

"She is inviting us to eat," explained Vic.

She brought over a steaming metal pan full of soup and ladled out carrots, onions, slices of potato, chunks of chicken and feet. Then, she ladled out broth with flecks of green. When she turned to get a pitcher of lemonade, I asked Vic, "Is this parsley?"

"*Cilantro.*"

It had more taste than parsley. We slurped as Romualda poured the lemonade. I left the chicken foot to last and asked Vic how to eat it. He grabbed one from his bowl and bit off the fingers. After chewing, he held up the remainder to show me a bone. "Some people put this whole piece in their mouth and spit out the bone. Others hold the end and suck the meat off. It's up to you."

Romualda watched and said, "*Te va a gustar, fuego.*"

"She said…"

"I'll like it. I understood." I held and sucked. It tasted like a chicken flavored gummy bear. Romualda smiled.

The second course consisted of homemade corn tortillas heated on a round piece of metal that Vic called a *comal*. They smelled sweet. She placed a cotton towel on a plate and stacked hot tortillas on it before folding the end of the towel over to keep them warm. From another pot on the stove, she used a wooden spoon with holes in it to serve up some green stuff.

Romualda sat behind us near the stove and saw me staring. "*Nopales.*"

"It's jumping cactus cooked with onions and cloves. It's supposed to be really good for you chubby guys," added Vic before laughing again.

When I hesitated, she made an eating motion and said aloud, "*Más verduras y menos pasteles.*"

Vic laughed. "Did you understand?"

"She told me to eat."

"Yeah, more vegetables and less cake. Roll it into a taco and eat it with your fingers."

It was delicious. After we ate, we helped Romualda wash dishes even though she complained. She had a few extra uncooked *nopal* leaves. She set one bowl next to a stool. Sitting on the stool with another bowl between her legs, she put on thick gloves and grabbed a paring knife. She grabbed a leaf with one hand and sliced off the needles in seconds. Once she had filled the bowl next to her with clean leaves, she showed me how to filet them. Before we left, she gave me more *sabila* leaves wrapped in wax paper.

As I mounted my bike, Vic asked, "Are you interested in a paper route?"

"Sure. I had one back east."

"I deliver the Scottsdale Progress, the afternoon paper. We've had an open route for a few weeks and I'm tired of delivering two routes. Meet me behind Skaggs at the loading dock tomorrow at three. I'll introduce you to our district manager, Don Smith."

The next day I found Vic and three other boys seated under the Skaggs back roof overhang, rolling and rubber-banding newspapers while a man with sunglasses dressed in khaki pants and a short sleeved white shirt marked papers on his clipboard.

Vic jumped up. "Mr. Smith! This is the guy I told you about."

I shook his hand. "You had a route before, right?" he asked. Before I could answer, he asked, "Did you collect?" I shook my head. "Every jackass thinks he's got horse sense. We can teach you. What's your name?"

"Jack Colter."

"Vic. Take Jack with you on your route for a day or so until I meet with Jack's parents. I'll deliver the route until then." Turning to me, he said, "Talk to your parents. Here's my card, I'll be glad to stop by your house to talk to them and sign some papers. Maybe we could meet sometime this week. Let me jot down your number."

I helped Vic roll papers and load his canvas bag. The bag fit over the handlebars and since the Progress was a thin newspaper with two sections, a load of thirty papers didn't weigh much. "I have an extra bag at home. I'll give it to you. Once in a great while, the bundle of papers come with plastic bags if it's expected to rain. Then we slip the rolled paper into the bag."

He explained that the very first thing to do in the afternoon was to count your bundle and check the number against your collection book: A stack of cardboard cards held together with two giant metal rings that opened easily. Each card had the customer's name, address and phone number on it. At the bottom were perforated tickets with dates. When the customer paid, you pulled off the correct date to give to them as a receipt.

"When do you collect?" I asked Vic as we pedaled past giant empty lots south, towards my neighborhood.

"I like Saturdays but that's up to you"

Both his route and mine covered one quarter mile wide by one half mile long. Vic explained that we weren't allowed to put newspapers in mailboxes and generally threw them near the front door. My first throw was bad and I had to go back which made Vic laugh. "You'll get better."

Two nights later, Mr. Smith came to our house to explain everything. Since my dad had delivered papers as a child and I had already had a route, the discussion was short and amiable. My mom served coffee and cookies while they filled out papers and he handed me my collection book, saying, "When you collect, don't be high falutin."

Over the next few days, Vic reviewed the steps; count newspapers, check the number against the latest collection books records, how to roll, how to load, how to deliver, how to collect. "Buy a cheap squirt gun at Skaggs," said Vic. "Load it with lemon juice and water. If a dog chases you, aim for their eyes. They'll stop and it won't blind them."

"Does that happen much?"

"No, but sometimes a dog can get out. Luckily, they usually bark."

We also talked about sports. Vic talked about flag football which was the first school sport of the year. "Yeah, you should try out," he told me.

"I really like basketball."

"Well, that's the next sport. We have an A team which is all eighth graders and a B team for seventh and eighth graders. We play five schools during a season. It's fun."

The next afternoon, Mr. Smith waited for me at the newspaper drop-off. "Let's store your bike in the back of my station wagon. I thought I'd drive you through the route today. Just load up your bag and set it in the middle of the front seat and we're ready to go. Brains in the head save blisters on the feet."

He helped roll the papers and we both ended up with inked stained hands. Since he had delivered the route, he offered great insights. "Mrs. Crabtree is an elderly widow. Make sure her paper is thrown by the back door, not the front. Here. Use this pen and take a note on her card. Some folks have good points but jab you with 'em like spurs."

He also explained how a few of my customers had installed metal cylindrical newspaper holders under the mailbox. "If it reads 'Scottsdale Progress' you can put the paper in it. If it reads 'Phoenix Gazette' or 'Arizona Republic' don't put the paper in it."

At one house, he stopped. "This gentleman must work two jobs. He's hard to reach for collections. Try calling him to set an appointment. Generally, if a customer is three weeks in arrears, you can cancel their account by calling the main office but that's up to you. You're paying for the papers."

He stopped at another house. "This family has a vicious bulldog in the backyard. It will slam against the gate trying to break it so that he can bite you. Be careful, youngster. You see that dog loose, skedaddle."

"Yes."

"Good, when collecting here always keep the squirt gun in the back of your pants, ready to go."

Collections were new and different. Some people complained about the placement of their paper. Others were all smiles and some even tipped me. The man in arrears apologized and explained that he had been out of town. When I knocked on the front door of the house with the vicious dog, someone inside yelled for me to go to the back door. I slipped my squirt gun in the back of my pants. At the back door, next to the gate, the bulldog smelled at the space between the gate and post. I saw its snout and recognized an English bulldog. The dog growled, then barked before throwing itself against the gate just like Mr. Smith had warned. With each smash, the metal hinges moved as if they were about to bend.

Someone inside was yelling, "Get the door!" I saw the doorknob move with hesitation before the door opened. Two small twin sisters in matching dirty dresses looked at me. From behind them I heard, "Come in!"

As I stepped into the kitchen/dining room, I smelled a familiar stench. There was a giant confederate flag hung on one wall and a table over-flowing with stacks of pamphlets. Off to my right I heard, "Over here!"

In the tiny living room, Eric Wetzel, the boy who called Vic a "beaner", was seated on a chair in the middle of the room with the same purple wet mess on his head as my mother used to bleach her hair. Behind him stood a woman in blue jeans and a simple blouse covered by an apron. She had rubber gloves on.

"I'm the paperboy. It's collection time," I said and wondered what kind of boy would want to bleach his hair.

"Jewel! Please give this young man a dollar from the cigar box on the table," said the woman and one of the little girls ran over to fetch the money.

Those Who Are Gone

I was just beginning to memorize my route and get used to collections when the newspaper ran an article about the new school year. At home, my parents also received a letter explaining that Yavapai would host a Back to School Night. This was only the second year that it would have grades one through eight and we would be the second graduating class. The event was to be run at staggered times by grades

The very next day, my mother drove me to The Mister Shop at Papago Plaza to buy new blue jeans, cotton shirts, underwear and socks but on Back to School Night, my parents dressed up: my dad wore a tie and my mom wore earrings. The front of the school had a manicured flower garden. All the windows reflected the late afternoon rose colored sky. Each classroom's sink and water fountain sparkled. The rooms smelled sweet and had been waxed and buffed until the floors reflected the image of our shoes. All the green boards on the walls were brand new. The library was the equivalent of four classrooms, filled with books.

The auditorium was filled with hundreds of parents and children. The principal explained that bells would be used for the upper grades and parents were encouraged to move to the next class and meet all of the teachers, math science, social studies, English, shop, home economics, music, art and physical education.

After a brief welcome in the auditorium, we met my home room math teacher. The walls were covered with bulletin boards full of mathematical formulas. Jim Bridger, Jed Smith, Chris Carson and Eric Wetzel, the bleach blond, were all in my class. Vic ended up in another homeroom. But

Those Who Are Gone

Chucho, Cájame and Wuicho were all in my class as well. I didn't know any of the girls.

So, my parents got to meet the parents of all the boys I had been playing with all summer. Jim Bridger's dad had a nearly identical tattoo on his forearm as my dad: an anchor. They had both been in the Pacific fleet during the Second World War. I overheard Mr. Bridger say that his nephew was a member of the Marines and had been sent to Vietnam. The two men went silent.

Coach Esposti had a limp. When my dad met him, and they shook hands, he noticed that Coach had "U.S.M.C." tattooed on his forearm. "Pacific or European theater?" asked my dad.

"Pacific. Iwo Jima."

Eric's mother had rings under her eyes. She held a baby in her arms and the twins stood on either side of her, clinging to her dress. Mrs. Franke, our homeroom math teacher, offered her lemonade and cookies but Eric's mom explained, "I really have to go to the first-grade class. The twins start school this year but thank you for the offer."

A few of my Spanish speaking friends' parents did not speak English and relied on their sons and daughters to translate. The fathers were dressed in new blue jeans held up by wide hand crafted leather belts with large buckles, cowboy hats and cowboy shirts with snap buttons and cowboy boots while their wives wore simple print dresses like Romualda. Some couples walked hunched over, heads down with their hands in front of their bodies as if they were praying. Others stood tall.

The next morning at breakfast, my dad sipped his coffee, looking blankly. "Eight children…"

My mom nodded. "That's a lot of mouths to feed."

My brother Dan set down his toast. "What are you talking about?"

"The Chacon family. Jack's friend's family. There are ten of them. Wow! That's a big family," said my dad.

There were no cookies or lemonade on the first day of school. Each class began with a roll call and the teacher asked if we had a preferred nickname. The majority were names like Bob, Tom, Gary, Susy and Betty. It made us all smile to watch the teacher's faces when they heard nicknames like Cájame, Chucho, Tacho, or Wuicho.

"Mr. Jacobs asked, "How 'bout we call you Bobby?"

"Cájame."

"Bobby is a nice name."

"Cájame: C…a…j…a…m…e. We pronounce the "j" like an "h."

"Thank you, Cájame."

Then, teachers handed out books and recorded numbers so they would know who was responsible for each book. While they were recording one by one, they usually assigned some kind of test. In each class, the period always seemed to end quicker than expected. It was like time had speeded up.

The best part of the day was lunch. The ladies in our cafeteria began baking at four in the morning so that each day we had fresh sweet bread, cupcakes or cakes. They also served us meat, potatoes, noodles or rice and fresh vegetables. We had our choice of milk, chocolate milk or strawberry flavored milk. That first day, our homeroom teacher handed out cards to Chucho, Cájame, Wuicho and Roberta. When we lined up to enter the cafeteria, we paid in cash but they just showed their card.

At the end of the day, men in long sleeved white shirts that had underarm perspiration stains and wrinkled dark dress slacks stood on two corners of McKinley opposite the school. They carried side bags and as we passed, they handed us a pamphlet, smiling. "Take this home to your parents. New members are welcome." The man who handed me the pamphlet had oiled blond hair combed straight back. He wore work boots instead of dress shoes and as he turned to hand a pamphlet to the student behind me, I noticed that the hairs on the back of his neck were dark.

I walked my bike down the street, reading but it didn't make much sense. It began with biographical material about some missionary named John Birch, then spoke about someone else and finally ranted about communist infiltration, the evils of the United Nations and the dangerous Civil Rights movement.

At dinner, I showed the pamphlet to my dad. While eating, he read. Once done, he slowly closed it and pushed it across the table. "Jack, please throw this in the garbage. That's what it is — hate garbage."

My brother announced, "I got my draft physical notice in the mail"

"When is it?" asked my dad.

"In two weeks."

We were only in school for a few days when Coach Esposti held the first flag football team tryouts. I had never played. Coach had a clip board with our names on a sheet of paper and spaces for notes. It was still over a hundred degrees each afternoon when we slipped on tennis shoes and stripped off shirts except for Wuicho. First we did a lap around the fenced field over brown, dry Bermuda grass. After a water break, we divided into groups. A third grade teacher assisted. They lined us up and timed us on fifty yard dashes. They had us throw and catch a football. We lined up and they asked us to rush Coach Esposti as if he were the quarterback. An assistant hiked him the ball. There were notes and more notes.

The only thing I really liked was rushing the passer, especially when Eric played quarterback. He always seemed to move in the same pattern so I began to anticipate this. Each time that I caught his flag before he threw the ball, he made these great faces and sometimes yelled or stomped his feet. Then, he always blamed the linemen for not blocking well enough. His line included Wuicho, Cájame, Chucho and Tacho, the same boys he called names only a few weeks before. I had learned some new Spanish words and whispered. "*Derecha*" if I wanted them to move to the right or "*Izquierda*" if I wanted them to move left. It's pretty easy to rush with help like that.

That's a pretty limited sports vocabulary compared to my buddies. Vic out-ran everyone. Jim also ran fast. Jed, Chris and Cájame could catch and run in zig-zags that made it almost impossible to grab their flags. Wuicho could block anyone. Sometimes, he knocked people down. I did not seem to fit in well.

At dinner I served up more vegetables and skipped dessert.

"Are you feeling all right?" asked my mom.

"I feel slow and fat."

"You're not fat, just chunky. You have heavy bones," said my mom.

My dad kept his head down and said nothing.

At the Thursday try-out, Coach Esposti told us, "Tomorrow morning I'll post a list on my door of those who will represent Yavapai in flag football. If there is a B next to your name it means that you will play on the B team. An A after your name means that you will play on the A team. I want to thank all of you for coming out. The school district limits the number of players. If you are a seventh grader and have no letter after your name, please keep being active and try again next year. If you are an eighth grader, keep playing hard. The high school football team has more members. You are all developing."

The next morning, I arrived early.

There must have been some kind of a typographical error: my name had an A after it which got me giddy enough to be playful during math class. Mrs. Franke asked a simple question and when nobody answered, she turned her back to write on the greenboard. The tall girl sitting in front of me had just started wearing a bra which was very visible under her white cotton blouse. I grabbed the back of her blouse and pulled the bra strap back like a slingshot and let it go. Without hesitation, Mert, the tall girl, turned and swung, landing a hook on my cheek and immediately whipped around in her seat and crossed her hands on the desk.

I probably had a silly look on my face. "Mr. Colter!" asked Mrs. Franke. "Is there a problem?"

"No, ma' am."

"Good." Mrs. Franke turned her back on us again.

Mert whispered, "You have an older brother, right?"

"Yes."

"I have five."

In our social studies class, Mr. Jacobs handed out a pamphlet with the title "Our Constitution." He explained that the State of Arizona Congress had passed a law requiring schools to introduce courses about our own government. "So my first question is, 'What is the U.S. Constitution?'"

Larissa Thompson, a popular girl in school and the daughter of an air force colonel, raised her hand and called out, "It's sacred."

"Some people think so but what exactly is it?"

"Isn't that what July fourth is all about?" asked another student.

"Not exactly," said Mr. Jacobs. "Has anyone played the game Monopoly? Raise your hands." Hands went up. "Before playing you read or someone read to you the rules, right?"

There were nods.

"The U.S. Constitution is the rule book of how our government works. It defines the parts of government, explains their purpose, defines how people are chosen to run the government and also defines citizen's rights and responsibilities."

"In Monopoly, there are several ways to play the game," said one student.

"The constitution can change. It's called an amendment and how to do that is also defined."

"It says here that slaves only counted as three fifths of a person. What does that mean?"

"That's definitely a good question for another time."

English class also began with early Americana. We read a novel titled *The Scarlet Letter* about a scandal in colonial America. A young married woman, separated from her husband, becomes pregnant. The Puritan penalty is to brand her on the face with letter "A" for adulteress. However, the townsfolk decide to make her embroider the letter on the breast of her dress and imprison her. The story follows her life and that of her estranged husband and lover.

Those Who Are Gone

The first question was, "I thought Puritans were the good guys who ate turkey and corn with Indians."

Wuicho said, "They didn't eat with the Yaquis."

"They didn't eat with the Pima either," said Chucho and the class laughed.

"The tribe they ate with no longer exists," said Mrs. Snead and we all went silent.

Someone finally asked, "Why? How?"

"Time's about up for today."

Shop was more down to earth, especially for youngsters like me who had never used any tools, never built anything. Jed Smith's dad who worked at Weyerhaeuser had all kinds of tools. Jed was already making beautiful wooden bowls on a lathe which could be dangerous. Gailen Neville didn't follow directions and his project flew off the machine, hitting him square in the face. If he had not been wearing the facemask, he might have had a rearranged smile. Jim Bridger's dad had tools too. He made this incredible chest for the foot of a bed. I actually saw Chris take apart a broken radio at home, lay it out on the floor and then put it all back together with a few new pieces here and there and made it work. My dad's tools were trays, chemicals, an enlarger and cameras.

Our first project was a wooden radio using wound copper wire to act as the receiver. Mine worked but it looked nightmarish as it had fallen from a considerable height and crashed on concrete. I really wanted to create something useful but more pleasing to the eye.

Mr. MacIntyre approved my idea to build a simple box with a sliding top. This time, I drew it all out first with dimensions and thought about materials. I used the electric sanding belt to make sure that each piece matched perfectly. I used the electric router to cut the slot for my sliding top and an electric jig saw to cut the sixteenth inch thick white Formica top. For nails, I used a nail set to make sure there were no hammer marks and also recessed the nails so the hole could be puttied. A clear varnish was applied with a very high quality brush so I didn't have to worry about stray hairs sealing themselves into the finish. After drying, this was steel-wooled down for another application of varnish. Four coats made it shine so well that I still have and use the box sixty years later.

The wood working helped by offering a calm time to consider all those questions, lots of pubescent questions. Action also helped. We had physical education on Monday, Wednesday and Fridays. During the flag football season, boys played it during class so that everyone had an idea of the basics, even if you were not on the school teams. We practiced on Tuesdays and Thursdays with games on Friday afternoon in place of last period physical education class.

Our first flag football practice was like a class. Coach sat us all down and explained that for the first week, we would concentrate on improving general skills in small groups. He introduced us to three other teachers who would assist. "Please follow their directions as I know you would mine. They've all played football and know what they're talking about. The drills will be for both offense and defense because you may play both. Next week, we will continue to work on skills but will also be practicing offensive and defensive plays."

One of those drills was called the "gauntlet." Coach laid out the four corners of a square with orange cones. On one side, the coach lined up four boys wearing the Velcro flag belts. Facing them about five yards out was an opposing player who would concentrate on the first in line who was the running back. When the coach handed the running back the ball, he was supposed to run forward zig-zagging while the facing player slid back and forth concentrating on his bellybutton while he tried to grab a flag and throw it down so the official could see it.

"Toll Booth" was another game to practice pulling flags. Cones were set out like a triangle. The point was five yards from the other two. Four players lined up single-file behind the two cones and would try to run by the single defensive player without him grabbing their flag or flags. They ran one after the other so that the defender was in constant motion.

"Shadow" was a blocking drill. Coach lined up three linemen. Facing them were two defenders getting ready to rush. The blockers could not use their hands or elbows but could raise their arms chest level with fists touching to make contact with the defender's chest. So the offensive line had to practice sliding while the rushers practiced evading them.

"Flagorama" was similar to "The Gauntlet" with a square marked with orange cones. Five players wearing flag belts were spread out. When the coach blew the whistle, a free-for-all started. Each player tried to pull as many flags as possible. If their own flag had been pulled but they had someone else's, they replaced their flag. After one minute, the player with the most flags won.

Since it was still plenty hot, we had frequent water breaks and probably ran for about thirty five minutes of the hour practice. We also took salt pills to help us retain more water.

Bermuda grass was the worst. During the hot months, the grass died. The seeds had three prongs, like stickers and each time you fell, you were covered with them, tiny thorns stuck in your arms and legs.

Vic, Chucho and Jim were the best at evading flag grabbers. Vic was the most amazing because he seemed to have different gears.

He would often slow down, and wag his hips which made the flags wave, then speed up. He especially liked tricking Eric who threw a couple of fits. Once coach had to pull Eric out of the drill. I asked Vic what the switching gears was all about.

"That's what Jim Thorpe used to do."

"Who?"

"An Oklahoma Indian who was an All-American football player, two-time Olympian, a professional baseball player and a professional football player. His Indian team beat Army one year. Dwight Eisenhower was their halfback and when asked about Thorpe, he said, 'All I remember is that he was fast. Real fast.'"

Each Monday a half hour before lunch, Mrs. Franke had us all do math problems. She very quietly made hand signals to our Spanish speakers who went up to her desk. She handed them a card and then motioned for the next person. It was mysterious.

I hadn't paid much attention to Eric until the day our math teacher called, "Time" and asked me to collect a quiz we took. My dad had given me an expensive pen for school and it went missing. As I neared Eric's desk in back, he was still scribbling answers — with my pen. I grabbed it right out of his hand.

"That's mine" and I slipped the pen into my chest pocket. He jumped up and kicked me. Luckily, his kick was off. He kicked me on the inside of my thigh. I took one step forward and smashed his nose with an overhand right that knocked him down. He was so stunned that he fell back down as he began to get up which gave our teacher time to step between us.

"Stop! Stop!" She separated us and gave Eric a tissue to wipe his bloody nose. Then she told him to sit down by the door outside.

After a call on the intercom, the Vice Principal accompanied us to his office where he sat us down next to the secretary while he waited for his witness, Coach Esposti, who went into the office and closed the door behind him. After a few seconds, he opened it and motioned for us to come in. While coach leaned against a wall, the Vice Principal told us to be seated in front of his desk.

Eric immediately said, "Please don't call our parents. My stepfather will beat me again…" and started to cry.

The Vice Principal looked at me. "Do you have anything to say?"

"He stole my pen. When I took it back, he kicked me."

"We can't have this sort of nonsense in my school." He stood up and walked slowly to his waist-high bookshelf, grabbing a thick wooden paddle with holes drilled through it. "Do you know why it has holes?" We didn't answer. "So I can hit harder." He pointed to me. "You first." He hit the paddle on his hand a few times as I walked over to the bookshelf. "Lean over and touch the wall," he said. "One, two, wait." He took the back of my untucked shirt and folded it up to expose my pants. "Three!"

I didn't move but he didn't repeat so I asked, "Is that it?"

"Get out of my office. I'll be calling your parents about suspension smart aleck."

Back in the classroom, I sat down slowly without a word. My backside was sore. When Eric came in, his face was still flushed from crying and a new piece of tissue stuck out of each of his nostrils.

"Please take out your text book and turn to page seventy-five. We are reading silently."

After my route, I found the table set and the family seated. "Someone's in trouble," said my brother.

"Sit down, son. Tell us what happened in school today."

So, I told them the whole story. "The Vice Principal mentioned suspension. I have a football game tomorrow."

My dad wiped his palm across his face, looked down. "There'll be no suspension. It's called self-defense. The next time, meet him at least one block away from the school grounds after school." Then he looked up at my brother. "Dan, after dinner teach Jack how to throw a better punch. That thief shouldn't have been able to get up."

Arriving early the next morning, Vice Principal Beard was the street crossing guard. Wearing the harlequin green vest over his dress shirt and tie, holding a stop sign, he did not look so menacing. "Good morning Mr. Beard." He ignored me.

Eric was missing-in-action. While talking to my classmates in the hall, Larissa ambled up. "Good morning, Jack," she said and smiled. In class we all did our work and during recess, Coach Esposti called over Vic, Chucho, Cájame and Wuicho. Afterwards, they explained to me that Eric was going to start as our quarterback but in his absence, Vic would step in and coach had some strange twists to the plays we had run.

Those Who Are Gone

    This was a home game. We were already warming up on the sidelines when the team from Supai arrived on a large yellow bus. The teachers had used cones and chalk to set up two parallel football fields fifty yards long by thirty yards wide for the A and B teams.

    Teachers led the lower grade students out. They had set up a staggered schedule so that the first through third graders watched for twenty minutes, the fourth through seventh watch for twenty minutes. Some of them held little handmade signs which they must have done as a class project.

    Our coach shook hands with the Supai coach and they smiled and talked for a moment before he limped back to our group and handed out blue vests to pull over our white t-shirts and adjusted our flag belts. Vic and Wuicho were our captain and co-captain for the coin toss which we lost.

    The other team opted to receive and Chris kicked off. It was a short run and our regular defense took the field. Wuicho and Chris were our rushers. Jed, Jim and Vic played linebackers with Vic in the middle while fast Chucho and tall Cájame played safeties. They tried a long pass on the first play which Cájame intercepted and ran back about twenty yards. We ran mostly running plays for the first half while they continued to throw. Our coach substituted freely and I got to play rusher and middle linebacker in spurts.

    At halftime the score was 21 to 14, Supai ahead. While we drank water, coach told us that we would be changing the plays a bit. On our first play, Vic rolled out as if he were going to run and then threw a five yard pass to Chris who caught it in stride and lost a flag immediately. The next play was the mirror image with Jim catching a five yard pass and eluded the defense to pick up ten yards. On the third play, Wuicho lined up in the backfield instead of as center.

Tacho took his place on the line. Wuicho was alongside Cájame which looked like Mutt and Jeff in the funny papers — the tall and short of our team, with Vic behind them. As soon as the ball was hiked, Cájame led, yelling and waving his wing-like long arms. One defender seemed to be surprised and slowed as they passed, Vic behind his two blockers. A few yards out Wuicho decked a linebacker and Vic took off in that second gear, wagging his hips to make the flags flutter. Touchdown!

It was a fun game which we won 35 to 21. We were in complete control and Coach Esposti began changing our positions. He even had Jim play quarterback in the fourth quarter. Afterwards, we lined up to shake hands before all running to the water fountains to drench ourselves. We were sopping wet with sweat, covered with dirt and dry Bermuda grass stickers.

Before we dried off with white towels that the coach threw to us, Larissa came by with two of her girlfriends. "Hello, Vic. Nice game."

Eric came back to school the following Wednesday. He had a black eye that was starting to turn yellowish. I gave him a head nod and he nodded back.

The paper route had become easier. My customers knew me and I knew their likes and dislikes. Mr. Pudmarski wanted the paper exactly on his front door "welcome" mat. Mrs. Hunsberger was an old widowed hoarder whose front door was blocked by surplus furniture and boxes so she wanted her paper at the back door in the carport. When I knocked to collect, she often greeted me with, "I'll pay you one dollar extra if you move some boxes for me." Inside there was not much visible furniture because everything was covered with stacked boxes. Even her hallways were lined with a stack so that you had to turn sideways to get through.

Mr. Tomlin worked nights. He always left his payment in an envelope under the front mat so that I wouldn't knock. I just opened the envelope, took out the money and replaced it with his perforated ticket.

I started taking a rag in my paper bag after my mom complained about the ink stains on my trousers. I had been wiping my sweaty hands on them and the ink was hard to get out.

Eric's house became the last delivery on my route. One time, I heard a different voice inside yelling, "Get the door."

One of the twins opened it a crack and I heard that same voice yell, "Well, come in, damn it."

At the kitchen table sat the same man who had handed me the hate pamphlet on the first day of school. This time he was dressed in an old school undershirt, washed out blue jeans and the same work boots. He hadn't shaved in a few days and his arms, exposed chest and back were covered with tattoos. He had skulls, devils, demons and the iron cross visible while he stapled together more pamphlets.

"Paperboy."

"Louise! Louise! Bring my wallet."

Mrs. Wetzel walked out wearing jeans, blouse and an apron again. She carried a baby and the twins, on both sides, clung to her legs. Mrs. Wetzel had a yellowing black eye like I had seen on Eric only weeks earlier. She placed the wallet on the table. Mr. Wetzel took out a dollar bill and handed it to me. "Take a cookie as a tip, kid." On the table was a plate with store bought cookies. "Go ahead. You earned it."

"Thank you," I said and skedaddled out the door, pedaling down the street as his English bulldog rammed itself into the gate. I threw the cookie into the gutter.

I'd been saving my money and found a cassette tape recorder at Skaggs. My mom drove me to the Thomas Mall in Phoenix where I bought a tape recorded Spanish lesson. On the way home, we stopped at a used bookstore and bought a Spanish textbook. I began to study just before bedtime each night. Sometimes I used a flashlight to read the book late into the night.

I liked that the vowels in Spanish had only one way to pronounce them. In English, the letter "O" has thirty-two pronunciations. Spanish is phonetic and as I learned words with the tape, I could simultaneously read them. There were a few curve balls like the double "R" which sounds a bit like a machine gun. You have to learn how to roll your "Rs" which means your tongue has to get used to moving differently. The double "L" in Spanish is pronounced like a "Y." There's a letter "N" with a curved line over it and it sounds a bit like an "N" followed by a "Y." Those are the big differences. The only really hard part is that you can place a verb just about anywhere in the sentence which takes getting used to. Unlike English with the train approach: subject followed by verb followed by modifiers, Spanish is more like a collage which evokes a feeling as well as a thought.

On Saturdays, we still often rode bikes as a group. Vic made a regular run about three quarters of a mile north to a Mexican produce store to buy things for Romualda. It really felt great to pull up on our bicycles and read the signs in Spanish.

"Big sale today!"
"Half price on *nopales*."
"Elderly discount."

Inside, I saw an unfamiliar word on a sign and asked the cashier, "What does *sabrosisimo* mean?"

He smiled broadly. "It means the most delicious."

We left the store with two bags of fresh produce and as we walked out, Eric rode up. "Hey chief! Did you get a job as a maid?"

I looked at Vic and said. "*Las manzanas son sabrosisimas, ¿Verdad?*"

Vic nodded. "*Sí. Me encantan.*"

"You pull that in a game and you'll never get the ball again," said Eric and he pedaled away.

He was misinformed on lots of topics. Coach Esposti now played him exclusively on defense. Vic and Jim traded in and out as quarterback. Sometimes Jed stepped in as quarterback. We were undefeated without Eric as quarterback.

It was much the same with romance. Larissa made it a habit of surrounding Vic with girlfriends at recess to ask silly football questions. Eric usually showed up, running one hand through his longer blond hair while making snide comments.

That's not to say that we and our teammates had it all figured out. Another Saturday, a group of us rode to Hole in the Rock together and on the way home we divided up because everyone had different destinations. Jed, Wuicho and I rode south towards the Tempe border and stopped at a drive-in store. We all bought a soft drink and walked outside towards a curb. As we sat down, Jed pulled a candy bar from his pocket, smiling.

"You didn't pay for that," said Wuicho.

"Nobody cares about a little candy bar," responded Jed.

"You don't understand," said Wuicho getting up. "They'll blame me, not you. I'm an Indian."

Jed marched back in the store. "Hey! I forgot to pay for this." He placed a quarter in the counter.

A few days later, Mr. Jacobs, our social studies teacher, handed out permission slips. "Please have your parents sign this to give their permission for you to attend a field trip. We will be bussed to Phoenix to visit an archeological site called Pueblo Grande located on the shores of the Salt River about five miles from here. We will depart at eight thirty and be back by lunch."

"What's an archaeological dig?"

"Arizona State University will have students digging in the ground for really old things. That area was a city more than one thousand years ago."

"Were those the Yaquis or the Pima?"

"It was built by people before. We only know them by the name Hohokam."

"Like the school."

"Exactly. You will meet the City of Phoenix archaeologist who manages the dig and the site. Phoenix was the first in our country to employ an archaeologist."

"What does an archaeologist do besides dig holes?"

"They make maps of where buildings used to be. They put old broken things back together like puzzles and try to figure out what they were used for. Sometimes, they even learn ancient languages to help read old things."

"Did the Indians write?"

"Here in the Southwest, some groups had symbols that they used like writing. Farther south in Mexico and

Central America, Indians did write and left books and buildings with writing on them."

"So, we weren't the first here?' asked Larissa.

"No. Remember to pack a container of water and a snack. There are no facilities at this site other than outhouses."

The day before our field trip. Eric tried to cut in front of Chucho, the smallest eighth grader, at the lunch line.

Vic stepped in and put a hand on Eric's shoulder which Eric immediately brushed off.

"Back off, chief."

They were on the ground wrestling in seconds. A teacher ran over, broke it up and marched them to the office. There were no suspensions but each received a swat and both were prohibited from attending the field trip. They would stay behind in the library to take hours and hours of math quizzes.

The trip to Pueblo Grande took much longer than it does today. Curry Road had two lanes that wound through a small mountain pass. The site itself was a giant piece of desert, some fenced off.

The City of Phoenix Archaeologist, Dr. Emil W. Haury awaited us at a cyclone fenced gate. Wearing khaki jungle shorts, white socks, ankle-high construction boots, a long-sleeved blue cotton shirt with underarm sweat rings, a red bandana around his neck, sunglasses and a wide brimmed straw hat, he looked more like a movie-style bwana than a doctor of something or other. He smiled and waved to

Mr. Jacobs. When the two met, Dr. Haury hugged him. We formed a semi-circle around them, under a huge tent roof.

"Boys and girls, this is Dr. Emil Haury, the City of Phoenix archaeologist and a professor at the University of Arizona in Tucson," said Mr. Jacobs. "This site was donated to the City of Phoenix in 1924 because of its unique historical importance. The city was the first in the nation to hire an archaeologist. Dr. Haury has been studying this for years."

The doctor took a step forward. "Mr. Jacobs forgot to tell you that he was my student a few years ago. Of course, one of my great students. I've recently set aside my administrative duties at the museum and have begun a sabbatical from the university because we are conducting Hohokam studies south of Chandler on the Gila River. I'm here today to help the students of my student and it is a great pleasure to meet you all."

"What's a sabbatical?" asked someone.

"It's like a vacation from work to do other work. I'll be supervising that dig at Snake Town, south of Chandler."

A hand went up. "What kind of hat is that?"

"It's a Mexican hat. They make the best straw hats," he replied and our Spanish speaking students smiled.

Cájame nudged Wuicho. "*Te dije.*"

"Long ago, there were no national boundaries like we know them today. The Valley of the Sun was inhabited by a people we know as the Hohokam who built this city and other towns along the Salt and Gila Rivers. They also built hundreds of miles of canals to siphon off river water for irrigating crops. You are familiar with many of them because after the construction of the Roosevelt Dam, new modern canals were built for the same purpose, many right on top of the prehistoric ones."

Those Who Are Gone

"What did the Indians grow?"

"We're just finding out. We know that they grew corn, squash, beans, *chiles*, pumpkins, tobacco and cotton."

A hand went up. "Why did they build on top of the old?"

"The Hohokam system was engineered to follow the form of the earth so that the water would flow without pumps. It still works today. Our ancestors just expanded the canals and used concrete liners to make maintenance easier."

Another student asked. "When did this happen?"

"The modern canals were begun in 1878. We believe the Hohokam began building their ancient system about 1,500 years ago. There was a horrible drought about 700 years ago and they began to leave."

"Where did they go?"

"We don't know for sure but suspect that they headed south to what is today Mexico. When the Spanish *conquistadores* arrived in 1540, they met what might have been the descendants of the Hohokam, the Papago and Pima. They asked Native Americans who built the canals, towns and city. The Pima and Papago responded in their language, 'Hohokam' which means, those who are gone. Yavapai is only about a quarter mile west of the Pima Reservation. Anyone here a Papago or Pima?"

Wuicho and Roberta raised their hands. Wuicho said, "Pima. Did you find a jade ring?"

"We've found several."

"One of them was my great, great, great, great grandmother's."

Everyone laughed. Still smiling, Dr. Haury asked, "Any Yaquis?"

Chucho, Tacho and Cájame raised their hands.

Dr. Haury tipped his hat. "The Pima were using the canals to grow food. The Yaquis have a long history of migrating north and south but the greatest migration north happened between 1880 and 1930. They helped to build and maintain Scottsdale's section of the canal system. Do any of you have family or friends who worked on the canal?"

Again, Chucho, Tacho and Cájame raised their hands. "A classmate of ours couldn't make it today but his grandmother came in 1928 and her husband worked the canal too."

"Why don't we take a look at what the Hohokam built 1,500 years ago? We have metal rods stuck in the ground with ropes on each side of a path. Please stay on the path and do not touch anything. This is an active dig. When we climb a little hill, you will see student archeologists on their hands and knees digging with special tools or maybe brushing dirt away with paint brushes. They are trying to carefully remove old things without breaking them. They may be inside of an area with strings like a checkerboard. This makes it easier for us to describe exactly where these things were found."

"Can we ask them questions?'

"Sure. Someone in this group might be tomorrow's archaeologist."

"Do they hire Indians?"

"The dig we're doing at Snake Town includes thirty-two men and women, all Pima or Maricopa Indians."

He led us to a tall adobe wall and stopped. "We will be following this path around and up. On top are old buildings on a giant platform surrounded by this wall built about 1,000 years ago. The bricks were made with wooden forms out of clay and set to dry in the sun…"

Those Who Are Gone

Chucho nudged Wuicho. "*¿Ya vez?* I told you. *Telo dije.*"

We walked and walked. Dr. Haury showed us mounds, homes, courtyards and even the remnants of their irrigation canals. By the time Dr. Haury waved goodbye, we were hot, sweaty, tired and hungry. The bus ride back was quiet but once we had our cafeteria lunch, everyone started to talk about what we had seen.

"Well, Dr. Haury said that the Hohokam went south. Isn't that where your family is from?" asked Mert.

"Those people grew cotton and spun cloth," said Chris. "That's amazing."

The teachers must have noticed our enthusiasm. They assigned a joint English/social studies project. We were to go home and talk to family, trying to put together a family tree. Mr. Jacobs showed us how one looked. "In three weeks, you will give a three minute presentation to the class about what you found out. If you wish to write to places for birth or death certificates, I recommend it. Be aware that they might ask for a dollar to cover the cost of mailing."

Mrs. Snead gave us examples of interviewing people for what she called "oral history." She handed out mimeographed sheets. "These are sample questions. Since you do not have tape recorders and the library does not have enough for the entire eighth grade, take notes. Your first questions are very easy. You will be working backwards: your name and birthdate, your brothers and sisters, your parents. Mr. Jacobs already showed you how your parents will be above you and your siblings on your graph. For your parents and grandparents, you want to know where they were born, when and what they do for a living. If they can tell you anything about the place they grew up in it could be very interesting. Remember to take notes."

49

"What if your parents don't speak English?"

"Can you understand them?" asked Mrs. Snead. Everyone laughed. "Good. Then translate to English. This is a valuable skill. When you get to this part, ask open ended questions. For instance, what was it like growing up? Let them tell you and nod your head. Say things like, 'That's interesting.'"

"What if they don't want to talk?" asked Roberta.

"They'll talk if you ask them. They want to share. We all want to share."

"In four weeks, you will make a three-minute presentation about something interesting you found out."

During dinner, my brother immediately said, "Remember crazy Uncle Alex? That guy was a winner."

"Shhh," said my mom. "Let's not talk poorly of the dead."

"Plus," said my dad. "I don't think that those are the kinds of stories the teachers are looking for."

After washing dishes, my parents and I sat down without my brother and we began on the simple part, trying to map out names and dates. Both my parents were pretty good with names but not so sure of dates. Now I understood why they had given us so much time. I mentioned birth and death records.

"I can help with that," said my mom. "I will start with my parents and your father's parents."

Flag football was more complicated. Coach Esposti couldn't play Eric or Vic in the next game because of the fight. Wuicho had a purple sprained ankle after stepping in a gopher hole during practice and Jim popped his knee during practice. Jed held his leg up in the air while Jim, laying on the ground, popped it back before wrapping it in an athletic bandage. He limped all week. We lost the next game in a closely fought, back and forth battle.

Mrs. Franke, our homeroom math teacher, was absent one Monday. Just before lunch her substitute, Mr. Anouilh, unexpectedly called the names of all our Spanish speaking peers. "I will hand out your welfare cards now" and he asked them to form a line in front next to Mrs. Franke's desk.

While eating, Vic said, "I hate it when substitutes do that."

"What?"

"Hand out those cards in front of everyone."

"I don't really know what the cards are for."

"Free lunch because our families are poor."

After lunch, the substitute marched us all over to the cafeteria where the cooking ladies and janitors folded and moved tables, swept and mopped floors.

"Follow me," he said and led us up the side stairs onto the stage where a pretty young lady in a dress stood.

"Thank you.

"Good luck."

"Please form a large circle around me," she said. "Now, count off numbers." Once we had done this, she said, "The odd numbers, please stomp one foot like this," and counted off as she stomped loud with one foot, "One. two. three, four, one two, three, four, one two three four."

I was an odd number and followed her instructions as did the others. Since the stage floor was made of wood, our stomping echoed.

"Good. When I go like this." She put her hands in front of her, together, nearly touching and palms down. Then she moved them out. We stopped. "You'll start when I motion like this." She held both hands in front of her about shoulder height with index fingers extended and moved them up and down.

Someone raised their hand. She immediately pointed to him and said, "This is a doing class, not a question and answer class. Now, even numbers, clap your hands twice on the second beat. Foot stompers!" She held her index fingers up, moved them down and counted off as they stomped. "One, two, three four, one two three four." Get ready clappers!" As she counted the two, she motioned but the clappers were off and we all laughed. "Let's try it again. Foot stompers! One, two, three, four, one two, three, four. Clappers! One now!, three , four, one now!" It sounded interesting.

"Folks. This is rhythm," she said "Let's add some notes a cappella which means voice and no instruments.

She dramatically raised her hands again and got that rhythm going and began to sing a song we'd all been singing since we entered school, " As I went walking, that ribbon of highway, I saw above me an endless skyway. I saw below me a golden valley. This land was made for you and me. Everybody! This land is your land. This land is my land from California to the New York island, from the redwood forest to the gulf stream waters, this land is made for you and me."

We all stopped, smiling. She smiled too. "You all sang great but you forgot to keep foot stomping and clapping. Everybody take a seat where you're at." She stepped to the middle of our circle, dragging a brown metal folding chair with "Yavapai" stenciled in white on the backrest. She sat down, crossing her legs.. "I'm Miss

Johnson, your music teacher. We will meet once a week for fifty minutes and over the next few weeks of my cycle at your school we will sing and dance. No books. No tests. No essays." Then she pointed at Chucho. "What do you think about that?"

"Sounds good to me."

"All I ask of you is that you try. I need to also warn you: nobody is allowed to make fun of anybody else. No exceptions. If you tease anybody, you will be sent to the office and Mr. Beard will deal with you. Now, let's go around the room. Please tell me your name and let me know if you play any instrument or if anyone in your family plays an instrument or sings or dances."

She had a clipboard with a roll sheet and could have used it to call names in alphabetical order but she chose not to. "We will meet each other in a clockwise fashion which means I'll start with you," she pointed to Chucho, "and then we will move in this direction. So, *¿Quién es Ud.?* Who are you?" There were whispers.

"*Me llamo Jesús Monguilla* My name is Jesus Monguilla.."

"Chucho, right?"

"Right." There were more whispers. "Please keep it down. Let's listen. Chucho, do you play an instrument?"

"I play a drum for the Easter Deer Dance celebration."

"So, you speak two languages and play an instrument."

"I speak three languages, ma' am."

"The third language is Yaqui?" Chucho nodded. "You are considered a well-educated person, Chucho. Thank you for sharing."

Then she moved right along and everyone was very interested in talking about languages and music. Once we finished the introduction, we practiced that song a few more times until we could sing, clap and stomp. Just before the bell, she thanked us as a group and explained, "That song was written in 1940 by a man named Woody Guthrie. Your parents know it well." The bell rang and she smiled. "See you next week."

Football practice involved a lot of running. That combined with the paper route and Romualda's suggested diet all had an effect: my pants were very loose and the belt four notches in.

At our first family meeting, my dad noticed the loose pants and told my mother, "Doris, would you have the time to take Jack to The Mister Shop this Saturday to get him some new pants, please?"

"Sure." And we continued with our own history. Envelopes had started to arrive in the mail. My mom stacked them on the dinner table next to my plate so I could open them as we could talk about it over dinner. Soon, we had names, birthdates and death dates for everyone on both sides of the family back to my great grandparents who all had immigrated from Europe between 1870 and 1900.

"Are you going to type this up, Jack?" My brother asked. "I'd like a copy." Then, he held up a card. "I must have passed the military physical. They classified me 1A for the draft."

"What does that mean?" I asked.

"We have military service. All young men are eligible. If called for duty, you must report," said my dad. "Let's hope for the best." He glanced at Dan before pulling out one of our encyclopedias and looked up "U.S. history" and we read together how there was a huge wave of European migration to the United States at that time.

My mom had also written to some relatives back east and letters from them started to arrive. Some knew my ancestors and described them. We placed the letters into an empty shoe box and even gave it a label: Family Letters.

I kept studying Spanish on my own and had learned about 100 words as well as useful questions like; What is this? How do you say…? Where is…? Who is…? How is…? Why do you…?

At recess and football practice, my teammates helped. I might point to my shoes and ask, :"¿Qué es?"

They'd correct me. "There are two shoes, so you ask what are those — ¿Qué son?"

"Got it."

If Eric was on the practice field playing safety behind me, I teased him by speaking Spanish to the other linebackers or rushers. For instance, I might say, "*Es el hijo de Tarzan.*" In Mexico, if someone believes they are the son of Tarzan, they are spoiled and stuck up. We laughed.

Sometimes, he lost his temper and started screaming and stomping a foot. Coach Esposti blew his whistle and called him to the sidelines for a play or two.

Just before our last game, Larissa handed out invitations to her birthday party to be held on a Saturday night.

An hour later, I rode up to Eric's house to deliver my last paper of the afternoon. I pulled up the drive to throw the paper and I noticed that the gate was ajar.

Their dog threw himself against it and charged. I flung that paper as hard as I could and it bounced off the dog's snout. "*¡Ay Chihuahua!*" I turned the handlebars quickly and the squirt gun slipped out of the empty bag, the bike jackknifed and I went down. The dog was on me. He bit into my calf, pulling and twisting as it growled. The bulldog was nearly half my weight and I couldn't even get up so I yelled for help.

Mr. Wetzel must have been seated at the kitchen table inside because he ran out barefoot, dressed in his undershirt and a pair of old blue jeans held up by a green webbed military belt. As he ran down the drive he yelled, "Down boy! Down!" but the dog ignored his command and kept twisting my calf. He grabbed the dog by its metal choke collar and pulled the dog's head up to choke it which meant my leg went up too with the dog snarling, growling and chewing so I screamed. He dropped the dog and pulled off his webbed belt which had little hooks on it to hold things and he beat the dog as he yelled, "Down! Down!"

The dog finally let go of my leg and Mr. Wetzel immediately grabbed that choke collar again and with two hands lifted the dog off the ground so that it was suffocating. Once the dog stopped making noises and trying to attack me, Mr. Wetzel put him down a few feet up the drive and dragged him towards the gate.

I looked at my calf. The pants were torn up. My white sock was bloody but I lifted the bike, got on and pedaled as fast as I could. Near my house, my calf began to throb. It was almost dinner time and my dad's car was in the carport. Inside, he was watching something on television when I came in, sat on a dining room chair and told him, "A dog bit me."

"What?" he got up as I took off my shoe and peeled off the bloody sock. He started to roll the pant leg up. I yelled. "Stand then and take down the pants."

"Sorry about the pants, dad."

That's when my mom walked in the room. "Doris! Bring me some hot water, a bar of soap, alcohol, cotton pads and some kind of wrapping bandage and tape." Without a word, she ran down the hall.

My dad cleaned the wound and patched me up the best he could but it wouldn't stop bleeding. "We need to take you to the emergency services at the hospital," he told me.
"Doris, could you please get Jack a pair of his shorts? That's smarter than trying to put long pants on."

By the time we got to the emergency room, blood was running down my leg again. The same nurse who inspected my gravel-bit arms, had me sit on an the exam table. He carefully removed our bandages while asking questions. When he heard dog bite, he asked another nurse to contact the police.

"This is going to require stitches, Mr. Colter."

"A lot?" asked my dad.

"We can do it here. No operation. The major muscles do not appear to be torn."

The other nurse walked in with a metal tray carrying a needle and syringe. "Jack, we're going to start with an injection of antibiotics. The other nurse will bring in the tools to stitch this up."

"I'm good."

"Mr. Colter. A policeman is in the hall to take a report. It's required. Jack will probably walk out of here before you're done."

The stitches were weird. There was a tiny prick but when he pulled the thread through, I felt that too. Once finished, he covered it with a gauze pad and taped it to my leg. "Ah! You're sprouting leg hairs," said the nurse. "Manhood can't be far away. What sports do you play?"

We talked about flag football and basketball. I was just telling him how I loved to watch Bill Russell outplay Wilt Chamberlin when he said, "All done champ." I started to get up and he held his hand up. "Whoa, whoa. Let's get your father in here to talk about recovery."

I saw my dad shaking hands with a uniformed policeman. "How we doin'?" my dad asked as he walked in.

"All done. Please take Big Jack here home to watch television for the rest of the evening, leg propped up a bit. He cannot play sports for at least ten days when we take the stitches out. Bring him back on the tenth day, we'll have the anti-rabies serum ready to go if necessary. Jack, your calf will be sore and bruised. Please just take it easy. You'll be as strong as ever in a few weeks, just in time for basketball."

I started to get up and again, he held me back. "You'll be leaving on crutches. We want you to use them for at least five days and try to stay off your feet as much as possible."

I had never used crutches in my life and just getting out of the hospital door seemed difficult. Getting into and out of the car was even more difficult.

At home, My mom set up a stool with a pillow in front of the television and gave me a bowl of ice cream. My dad explained to my mom, "Since the dog bit him on Wetzel's property, the police cannot quarantine the dog. Unless he has paperwork on the dog's vaccinations, he must watch it for signs of rabies. They gave me this pamphlet to share with Wetzel. If there are any signs during the next ten days, Jack will have to start anti-rabies injections."

"How many injections?" asked my mom.

"Thirty administered in his belly button. I'm going over to Wetzel's now to give him the pamphlet and let him know that we won't have a complete reporting on costs until the stitches come out."

My dad was home soon, "That guy is not a pleasant fellow," he said. "Did you ever taunt his dog?"

"No."

"What?" asked my mother.

"He claims that Jack has been taunting his dog. He did have paperwork though. The dog has been vaccinated against rabies. It's just a mean dog."

"Mr. Wetzel is the man who handed out the hate pamphlets outside my school," I told my parents

"Is his son the one you beat up at school?" I nodded. "You concentrate on taking care of that leg, Jack. I'll call your newspaper district manager to let him know that you will need a substitute for at least the next ten days."

"Vic might be able to do it," I said.

"That's up to the district manager."

I called Vic to let him know what happened and asked if Romualda might have more *sabila* leaves.

"I'll talk to her," he responded. "If she has some, I could bring them to Larissa's party tomorrow."

"Great. What are you getting Larissa? I don't know what girls like."

"My dad gave me a special card so she can get free lessons at the golf course where he works," said Vic. "Yeah, he said it wasn't easy because they've been giving so many free passes out to new officers from Williams Air Force Base."

"That's a good idea. I'll ask my parents."

My dad's idea was simple. "Just buy her a bouquet of flowers at the Papago Plaza florist."

"Roses," added my mother.

"Doris, roses are expensive. They sell bouquets of a variety of flowers for half the price."

My dad had to be at Turf Paradise the next morning because the horses were running. That meant that my mom had to drive me to buy flowers. As we pulled up to the shop with a picture window full of bouquets of all colors, my mom handed me a folded up twenty-dollar bill. "Buy red roses."

That evening, my brother drove me a few houses down to Larissa's. He pulled up the drive. "You need help?" He watched me struggle to get on the crutches. Then, got out and walked around, carrying the flowers. "Don't forget these. Call us if you want to come home early."

Larissa's mother answered the back door. She was surprised to see me on crutches. "A dog bite." I explained as I handed her the flowers so that I could negotiate the crutches. "This is for Larissa."

"Well, come on in, doll and help me find a vase for these." She held the door as I stumbled through, still not used to crutches. Inside, she rummaged through cabinets until finding a vase she liked, held it up and said, "This is perfect." She put the flowers in, added some water and then sprinkled drops on the petals. She set the vase in the center of the dining room table. "Now everyone will see them."

One of her five sons slid the arcadia glass door open. "Mama. We're having some problems with these lights."

At that instant, someone else knocked at the back door. "Jack, make yourself comfortable. Billy, get Jim and Tom in here to monitor the front and back doors."

"Yes ma' am." He slid the glass door.

Through the arcadia door, I saw her restring the patio party lights, straightening table clothes and shake her finger at two sons who were already playing table tennis.

Three girls accompanied by an older brother rang the front bell before Larissa's brothers came in, so I hobbled to the front door. It was Mert and two others. They came in giggling while the brother looked me up and down. "What's with the crutches?'

"Dog bite."

He nodded. "Get well soon. Hopefully my little sister won't have to beat you up again. I'll tell her to take it easy on you." He smiled.

More girls arrived at the back door where one of Larissa's brothers answered. They also came in giggling and asking where Larissa was. All the presents were stacked on the table with my flowers.

Larissa appeared. " Thanks for coming, Jack. I heard about the dog. Does it hurt?"

"I'm sore. Happy birthday."

"Come on outside with me," she said and opened the sliding door. Of course, she was whisked off to a corner to whisper and giggle with the other girls. There was a table full of bowls of chips, candy, dip, hot dogs and buns cooking on a grill, overseen by one of her brothers. I ate some chips and felt a tap on the shoulder.

"I brought the *sabila*," said Vic holding up a plastic bag filled with leaves. We should ask Mrs. Thompson to put it into the refrigerator."

"Where's the group? ¿Dónde están los amigos?" I asked. "Weren't they invited?"

"They didn't feel comfortable."

Something about Vic looked different. Then, I realized. "You shaved your caterpillar mustache. "

"It was my dad's idea. Romualda called it my pubic hair mustache."

"I'll be off of crutches by Tuesday."

"I'll tell Romualda. She might want to rebandage it."

Mrs. Thompson stored my leaves and handed me a soda pop. "There's a cooler full in the back under the table, doll."

Soon, the yard, kitchen and dining room were filled with adolescents, talking and eating off of paper plates and drinking soda pop from metal cans. A few of the boys began to play table tennis. Chris was beating everybody probably because he had a table on his patio. Vic was holding his own. Eric was on the opposite side of the patio, talking to Larissa, quietly while brushing his blond hair off his brow.

Mrs. Thompson ambled over. "Good evening, Eric. You'll have to excuse Larissa. Since she's the host, she has to mingle." And she took Larissa by the arm and led her over to a group of girls.

The table tennis group of boys had become boisterous as they competed. Quietly, Mrs. Thompson slipped into the house and returned with a portable phonograph and a stack of records. She put on a fast Beatles song. Heads turned. Smiles appeared. Girls grabbed boys' hands. Before the end of the song, most of the table tennis crowd had dispersed. A new crowd had formed around the phonograph. Girls looked at the records and discussed which to play next.

None of us danced very well but with the fast music, you could bounce or just act silly and nobody seemed to mind. Vic danced with Larissa and I noticed Eric off in the corner, gnashing his teeth. He saw me staring. I nodded and he turned his back to me.

Well, I couldn't move around fast enough to play table tennis and dancing on crutches didn't make sense but I didn't want to be rude and go home. So, I helped Mrs. Thompson in the kitchen. She sat me down on a chair and had me wipe plates dry after she washed. One of her sons came in running.

"Mama. We have a problem on the side of the house."

She quickly wiped her hands dry and nearly ran. I followed but with those crutches I certainly did not medal that event. On the side of the house, I found Mrs. Thompson literally grabbing Eric by the neck of his shirt and lifting him off the ground. He had been on top of Vic.

"You two boys will not ruin my daughter's thirteenth birthday party!" She told her son Tom, "Turn that hose on a bit. "You two wash your faces and hands. Here! Use the dish rag to dry off. You, Vic, will go back to the party first and ask Larissa to dance. While everybody is watching, you will go out and dance with someone else," she told Eric.

She turned and as she walked out, told some curious party-goers, "Nothing to see here. Just go dance, honey."

Everyone followed orders. The cake with flaming candles came out and we sang "Happy Birthday." Soon, we all had frosting mustaches.

"I want to thank you all for coming and making my birthday special. This is the first big party I've ever had," Larissa told us.

Mrs. Thompson stepped out from behind her and added, "Your rides have already started coming. Please check outside. If you need to use our phone, Tom will show you where it's at."

I called Dan but my mom said that he was in the shower and might be a few minutes. I helped Larissa's brothers clean. I asked Mrs. Thompson, "Where is Mr. Thompson?"

"Today he's Colonel Thompson on a flying mission."

"Where to?"

"Oh, we can't talk about that, dear. There's a war now."

I apologized for asking too many questions and she said, "It's all right. It's a good question." She shook her head and then looked far away. "These problems in Asia do not pass the smell test." Then she seemed to focus and looked at me. "Let's just say that Colonel Thompson is now flying home with an empty bay."

My dad drove me to school on Monday. My underarms were raw from the crutches and my mom had taped extra padding onto the tops. Although I had learned to navigate with them through doors and around things, it was still difficult to get in and out of cars while shouldering my book bag.

Before I could even hobble over to the office to turn in my doctor's note, a group surrounded me to hear the story. The same happened as I entered the classroom. I never realized how horrible crutches are. Each time we changed classes or even wanted a drink of water, I struggled. By lunch, my underarms were chafed, my shoulders sore and of course, the calf sore just like the nurse warned me.

Those Who Are Gone

During recess, I let Coach Esposti know that I'd be off of crutches tomorrow but couldn't play in the final game. He pursed his lips, then smiled. "You're still a member on this team. On game day, could you help me with my clipboard?"

My only real problems that day were lunch and shop. Standing in line on crutches was miserable. Inside, I realized that walking on crutches while holding a tray just was impossible. Mr. Beard was on lunch duty and he volunteered to carry my tray. In shop, I had never paid attention to how much we walked back and forth from one work area to another. Luckily, I was working on a sidewalk surfboard that required some filing, With permission, I pulled a chair up next to a vice, locked the board in and filed from a seated position which worked, sort of.

I was a good patient. My mom picked me up from school. At home she helped me to set up a stool near the dining room table so I could elevate my leg. I drank milk while she worked on the other half of the table, colorizing black and white winning circle photos with oil-based paints from tiny tubes. She used an old plate as her palette to mix paints and meticulously burnished the photo using cotton swabs and toothpicks. Each photo took two or three hours to colorize but race horse owners paid big bucks. She had done this for years and had no problem talking while she worked. I carefully removed the bandage and made a third *sabila* poultice. It felt strange not to have newspapers to deliver. My mom suggested some cream on my raw underarms.

Tuesday afternoon after school, I was officially off the crutches. I set them against the wall near the back door and rode my bike to Vic's where Romualda was watching Vic's siblings while he delivered papers.

"*Buenas tardes, Doña Romualda. Espero que estés bien.*"

"*Eww. Hablas muy bien, fuegito. Me han dicho que un perrito te mordió.*"

"*Era un perrote, doña.*"

Romualda let out a belly laugh. "*Pásate. Vamos a revisarla.*"

Vic's siblings were all huddled in front of a black and white television, watching the Wallace and Ladmo show. Vic's six grade sister waved silently. Romualda served me hot Moronel tea. I wore shorts, so it was easy to remove the bandage and see the stitched wound which was clean and thanks to the *sabila,* healing. She dabbed it with clean water and applied a paste of various leaves with a fileted piece of *sabila* covering it and all of this covered by gauze, taped down securely. Before I left, she gave me a bag of curative leaves and another small bag of tea leaves, telling me to drink the tea in the morning and in the evening.

Back at home, without a paper route, we worked on the family history after dinner. More letters had arrived and now I had better questions for my own parents. For instance, I found out that they met at the Art Institute of Chicago. My mom was on scholarship and my dad studied photography there with the G.I. Bill. He also tended a downtown neighborhood bar for his Uncle Al.

Our Wednesday music class was a bit different. Mrs. Franke marched us over. Ms. Johnson was seated at an upright piano. Aluminum bleachers were set up on the back of the stage.

Those Who Are Gone

"Good afternoon, Miss Johnson."

"Thank you for bringing them, Mrs. Franke."

"Class, have a seat on the floor, please."

Then she played a scale on the piano, singing, "Do, Re, Mi, Fa, So, La, Ti, Do." She continued up the scale, repeating and again before saying, "That's about as high as I can go. Let's see what you can do. Chucho! You first. Step over here next to the piano."

Once Chucho couldn't sing any higher, she took a clipboard off of the top of her piano and wrote something down. "Chris! You're next."

She tested all twenty-five of us in maybe ten minutes and like a magician, started to group us on the bleachers, standing up and giving us a number between one and three. "We are going to practice breathing. Don't tell me you can't because if that were true, you'd be dead." We all laughed. "Everyone clasp your hands in front of your tummies. Breath deep. In. Out."

She listened and watched. "Larissa! Stop talking and breath deep on my command, please. Cájame! You call that a deep breath?"

Soon, we were all breathing very slowly and deeply. "Now place your hands on the center of your tummy. Take a deep breath and push as you sing as loud as you can like this: Doooooe. Breath and sing!"

"If you are truly breathing deep, you should be able to sing a lot louder than you thought possible." We practiced this a few times before she explained our grouping. "You are grouped by how you naturally sing. We never ask people to do what they can't. That wouldn't be fair."

Then she passed out the chorus to This Land is Your Land. "You might know this by heart but just in case, here's a copy to read. We'll start with section one."

She stood before us like a *maestra*, hands up about shoulder height, index fingers pointing up. They moved up and down and the section one began to sing, "This land is your land, this land is my land…"

"Keep going."

"Section two!" She raised her fingers and started them in time with the first group. "And group three!" She again raised her fingers." Then she stood back and listened. "Tacho! I don't hear you!." He did not respond and she made the "all stop" sign. "Tacho, are you all right?"

"My older brother left for the army this morning."

"Maybe we should sing for him."

"Let's take it from the top." Miss Johnson made the "start" sign. Once finished, she smiled. "Folks, that was an example of point and counterpoint as well as beautiful harmony. Take a copy of this entire song that I have made for you on your way out. Good work! See you next week."

I can't tell you how everyone else felt but I was elated. The sound we made was unbelievable. I did not want class to end. Maybe others felt similar because Eric thanked her. Wuicho asked if we couldn't sing more. Larissa apologized for talking, all as we filed out.

What I didn't know was that Vic's dad had given him a used acoustic guitar for his birthday in June. He had been learning chords in his secret space under the house where it cantilevered over the creek. His music class was doing the same thing that we were. At the afternoon recess, he told me, "I can play that song on my guitar. Come over after school and I'll show you. I can deliver papers a little late today."

After school, we rode out the back gate, across the *arroyo*, over the bridge and up to the narrow gravel road. We stopped and gathered some rocks. As we headed to his

Those Who Are Gone

house, two dogs ran out barking. We stopped and threw stones until the dogs yelped and ran.

We greeted Romualda as Vic grabbed his guitar, hanging high on one wall, and we dashed out and around to his secret space, crawling into a room made of plywood just tall enough to sit in.

Vic tuned his guitar with a tuning fork which I had never seen before. It was made of metal: a handle that led to a "U" shaped twin fork. He tapped it on the plywood wall and placed the handle part on the guitar body. It let out a note. Based on that, he tuned his first string by turning a button high on the guitar neck until it matched the tuning fork note. Then, he depressed the second string on the fifth fret with his index finger, plucked the first string, and the second, adjusting the sound of the second to the first. He continued with each string.

"That song only has three chords and I already know them! You sing and I'll play."

"This land is your land…"

"Slower please."

"Right. This…land…is…your…land…"

He played and it sounded good. We practiced for a good while before we mounted our bikes. This time, we pedaled out the exit at McDowell Road, at the intersection of the alley was a used car dealership on one side and a lounge and drive-through liquor store on the other. There was a poorly dressed man slumped on a high curb drinking from a bottle covered with a brown paper bag.

As we passed, Vic called out to him, *"Buenas tardes, Señor de Silva."*

The man nodded without a word. "That's Wuicho's dad?"

"Yeah. Poor Wuicho is probably going to get beat tonight."

We stopped at 76th Street before parting. Vic explained that the district manager was delivering my route and that he had already stopped delivery to Eric's house. "He said that Mr. Wetzel is a jerk and that he could buy his paper at the store! I never heard him say that about anyone before."

That night I finished a pencil draft of my family tree going back to my great grandparents on both sides and showed it to my parents. They nodded before my mom brought out a drawing board, a wooden T-square, a wooden twelve inch ruler and some ink pens. "These are from school, a long time ago. Good thing I kept them."

First she taped the edges of a sheet of my lined notebook paper to the drawing board. Then, she looked at my draft and measured off some lines which she marked with pencil and finally rolled out a piece of transparent paper over it, cut and pasted this on top. She called this buff paper and neatly printed names and dates with the pen. "What do you think?"

"It's great," I answered.

She dramatically ripped the buff paper off, crumpled it and threw it on the floor. "Your turn."

Luckily, she had a roll of buff paper because it took quite a few tries before my version was almost as neat as hers. She nodded. "Well, that's half your project. Tomorrow you can begin to write down something to say. Three minutes should be about a page and three quarters of a second page."

"That's not as much as my last book report."

"It's not much, I agree."

For our last game after receiving the kick-off, Coach handed me his clipboard.

"Colter call out the starting offense. They're marked in yellow."

I called out the names and they took the field. Coach placed Jed at quarterback with both Vic and Jim as his backfield. This was a different look for us. Coach held up some fingers to denote the play. Jed nodded and went to the huddle. On the very first play, Jed and his backfield ran to their right with Wuicho pulling as their blocker. Jed was out front. Before passing the line, he lateraled back to Jim and blocked someone. As they ran, Jim lateraled to Vic and immediately blocked another opposing player. Vic did his Jim Thorpe hip shake and shifted to the next gear. He ran all the way for a touchdown.

While they were celebrating, coach yelled to me, "Call out the defensive starters, Colter. They're marked in pink." Then he motioned for the offense to get off the field.

This was the first time in three weeks that we played with almost a full roster and it showed. Our defense smothered them and our offense steam-rolled. At the end, our defense stood on the field looking at us on the sidelines and all screamed, "¡*Eh la moey*!" What a way to end a season! We won 42 to 14.

As the teams shook hands, I overheard Coach Esposti apologize to the other coach. "The boys got a little carried away. I'm sure you'll pay us back during basketball." They both smiled.

I was a good patient with a minimum of activity, drinking my tea twice a day and applying herbs. On the tenth day, my dad accompanied me to the hospital again where the same nurse greeted me.

"Let's see if you're ready to play Bill Russell." He had a tray with shiny tools next to the exam table where I sat. He removed the bandage. "Holy cow!"

"Is everything all right?" asked my dad.

"I've never seen this. The skin grew over the stitches. I'm going to swab the area with a local anesthetic called procaine so Jack won't feel discomfort."

He did that and had to use a pen knife to open the wound a tiny bit. With tweezers, he exposed a stitch and clipped with this long scissors, then pulled with the tweezers. Stitch by stitch, he cut and pulled. Once done, he swabbed on some antiseptic and covered it with a smaller bandage.

"Keep it covered with a bandage for a couple of days. You certainly did your work, Jack."

"Can I play ball?"

"Yeah, but you've lost considerable weight. Russell would just push you around."

My dad paid on our way out and collected a receipt. "I'll make copies of this and present all the bills to Mr. Wetzel. You need to call Mr. Smith about deliveries if you want to continue."

"He's already stopped delivery to the Wetzel's house and that was the only really mean dog on the route."

At school there was a break between sports but Vic spoke to several of us on the football team during lunch and made a proposal. "Why don't we have our own practices starting now?"

"We didn't do that with football," said Jed.

"It's hard to organize fourteen kids to meet. In basketball we can play one on one, two on two, whatever we want."

Those Who Are Gone

"Let's start on Saturday morning when it's cool," said Jed.

Our Wednesday music class was just as surprising as the first two. Miss Johnson had us practice the chorus of the song for a while but then began asking certain students to sing a verse. She had Chris sing a verse, followed by the group singing the chorus. Mert sang a verse followed by the chorus. She had everybody in class try a verse.

Just before the bell, she explained, "We have one more meeting to practice. Next Thursday evening the school will hold a Back-to-School Night. It begins with the parents coming to the cafeteria to hear a local pastor say an opening prayer. The principal will make a speech and then, we will perform this song before the parents go to the individual classrooms where your teachers will have refreshments and plenty of your work to discuss. Next week, I'll assign the verses but in the meantime, go home and sing!"

That afternoon, I rode my bicycle alongside Vic to the loading dock behind Skaggs. We counted papers, talked as we sat side by side rolling and rubber-banding. Then, we pedaled south a block before he turned right and I turned left.

Several of my customers came out when I pedaled up as if they had been waiting for me. Mr. Pudmarski was angry because his paper had not been placed on his welcome mat. Mrs. Hunsberger was angry because the paper had been left at her front door instead of the back door. "I'll pay you one dollar extra if you could move some boxes for me."

Mr. Tomlin ran out.

"Where you been, son?"

"A dog bit me and I've been on crutches."

"Ya got any scars?" I rolled up my pant leg. "Yeah, that's a good one. Make up a dramatic story for the girls. A bit of sympathy never hurts." He winked. "Oh, here's your dough. Nobody's been pickin' it up."

Led by Vic, we began on Saturday with a bicycle ride to the canal maintenance road behind Supai and without stopping, rode back to Yavapai. It was a nice cool morning and some of us wore sweat shirts, others wore long sleeved cotton shirts over our t-shirts. Our group included Jim, Jed, Chris, Chucho, Wuicho and me. Tacho and Cájame were working: Tacho at a butcher's shop cleaning and Cájame at a restaurant washing dishes.

Jim had a cool wrist watch, so he kept track of time while we jogged around the open field. Next, we did fifty yard wind sprints. For the first time, I was not last.

Finally, we jogged over to the concrete courts behind the cafeteria where we divided into two teams of three for some half-court basketball. With buildings on two sides, the bouncing ball on concrete echoed. The hoops had metal chain nets that had several variations of sound which also echoed. If the ball was thrown high, the chain clanged as it fell straight through. If the ball bounced off the shooting square marked on the backboard, there was a thud usually followed by a higher pitched clang. When the ball spun through, it sounded like a wind chime. If the ball merely hit the rim, there was a loud bong and the chain rattled.

We didn't have any plays, but were having a wonderful time trying to juke each other and shoot. We played to twenty and switched the teams around. Then, switched them again. We were all tired when Eric, Craig Pudmarski and Phillip Watson, all eighth graders, pedaled up on bicycles.

"Corn muncher! Can we play?" asked Eric.

Those Who Are Gone

"I've got to go collect," I said and started to walk towards my bicycle.

"I've got some gas lights to clean," said Jed and walked off the court.

Everybody has some excuse and we all rode in different directions.

On Monday, all eighth grade classes began to present their family findings. Jim held his framed family tree which noted ancestor back for two hundred years on his father's side and maybe one hundred years on his mother's side.

He tried to explain each generation's names, dates of births, death and occupation, but at the three minute mark, Mr. Jacobs said, "Jim, excuse me for interrupting but your time is up. Let's open this to questions."

"Did you draw that family tree?" asked Chucho.

"No. My dad paid a company to research all this a few years ago. I'm related to William the Conqueror."

Susana Murrieta volunteered next. She had a family tree on a large piece of black cardboard. The names and dates had been typed and over each was a tiny black and white photo. Mr. Jacobs hung it on the green board with special clips so that it wouldn't be damaged by tape or pins.

She was a descendant of a famous Mexican *bandido* named Joaquin Murrieta. She explained that he had migrated north to California after the Mexican-American War. The new, provincial government of *gringos* passed the "Greaser Law" to get rid of Mexicans. Murrieta led gangs to rob white miners. Called the Mexican Robin Hood, he was murdered at the age of twenty-three.

Vic had a hand-drawn family tree which covered about two centuries, mostly on his dad's side. He explained how the Yaquis farmed using canals to the Yaqui river, south of what is Guaymas. They actually met the first Spanish expedition, heading north to search for the Seven Cities of Gold. The Spanish had horses, armor and muskets while the Yaquis had bows, arrows and spears. The first encounter became the first battle, with the Spanish retreating. The Yaquis fought for more than four centuries against the Spanish and later the Mexicans from the Yaqui River basin and the mountains. At one point, the Yaquis seceded from Mexico to form their own country.

This was news to most and hands went up for questions. "I thought the Yaquis came here because they wanted a better life," said Mert.

"We wanted to live," responded Vic. "In 1896 and again in 1926, the Mexican government had an extermination program. In 1926 they used poisonous gas dropped from planes, 12,000 troops and artillery. Yaquis were sold as slaves and taken by cattle cars to work on plantations in the Yucatan. My grandmother Romualda only survived because she had gone downslope to visit her family alongside the river. When she made it back, her home was destroyed and her husband and three children dead. She headed north using secret paths that led to Tucson."

"She just walked across?" asked Craig Pubmarski.

"At that time, Yaquis were welcome as political refugees because of the genocide."

"How did she get to Scottsdale?" asked Mr. Jacobs.

"She was a field worker in Tucson, then Yuma before moving to Guadalupe where she was often bussed to Goodyear, Chandler, Scottsdale to work the fields. She met my grandfather who maintained the Grand Canal and they moved to immigrant housing on Osborne. Some of the buildings are still there. My father was their first born."

"Isn't your grandmother some kind of healer?" asked Chris.

"She learned to be a Yaqui *curandera* from her father in Mexico. Before the Mexican-American War, Yaquis traditionally traveled back and forth from Sonora to what is now called Arizona and California. So did the Pima. They helped Yaquis fight the Mexican government."

This ended up a history class that was never repeated in any public school I ever attended. The next three days of eyewitness reports taught me more about the People's History of the southwest than anything offered in school or on the screen. Nobody insulted our peers. We listened and asked polite, maybe ignorant, questions. We knew Vic and appreciated his honesty. There was no chest beating or recitals of nonsense like "Manifest Destiny." The combination of our field trip to Pueblo Grande and these stories by different people humbled us. Even Eric was silent.

Later that day, Coach Esposti set a timer for four minutes before asking for two volunteers. Vic and Eric volunteered, Coach nodded and asked them to stand under the basket while he explained.

"First of all, this game will be played only within the half court. Vic and Eric are "it." They will try to tag you. If they do, you must leave the court and sit down behind the half court circle. You may run around the court lines, the half court circle or the free throw and lane demarcations. So choose your places, boys."

Once we all took a spot and began running, coach told Vic and Eric, "Go get 'em."

Since we had been riding, running and playing for weeks, nobody from our group tired. Vic ran right out there and started tagging people who left the court. Eric seemed to get his feet tied up a few times but did all right.

As we ran, Coach Esposti talked to us. "We only have twelve players on this squad and will play in four eight minute blocks. Get ready to run."

The timer rang loud. "Colter, Smith: you're it. Let's go!" He reset the timer.

At the end of the second round, coach showed us how to do a lay-up and had us practice, running from either side of the free throw lane with him passing. After, he divided us into two lines on either side of a basket. "When I blow the whistle, the boy on my right side will dribble down to the center court circle while the player on my left continues to run straight. The player at half court will pass to the other, then cut towards the basket. The other player will pass it to the cutter for a layup."

Coach watched us run. "Faster."

On the second run through he yelled, "Faster."

Coach showed us six spots on the court that he had marked with a small dot of red paint: on either side of the basket near the out-of-bounds line and four on the key lines. Two of those were marked on either side of the free throw and the other two were halfway up towards the basket on the lane lines. He had a large metal cart with twelve basketballs. "Everybody grab a ball."

He divided us into two groups of six for either side of the court.

"Let's go. Practice those shots."

Ten minutes before the end of practice, coach had the two groups of six try something else. He lined up one player under the basket and one on each extreme side. Each man had a ball.

Those Who Are Gone

We were to dribble as fast as possible to the mid-court line, then turn and dribble in for a shot. The boys on the edges were to either use a two handed push shot or a jumper. The boy in the middle did a lay-up. Coach watched without a word.

After a few minutes, he yelled, "Now dribble with your other hand." Except for Vic, Jim and Chris, most of us went into slow motion. We looked a bit like wacko mechanical toys with rundown batteries, dropping the ball or weaving crazily to keep the ball under control.

After one set, coach told us to sit down and take a breather. "That wasn't bad. We'll keep working until we all become proficient. And you will. Please put the balls in the basket and see you next time."

School had an unexpected change. During the first six weeks, we had had an art teacher who worked with us in our own homeroom. She had us draw with crayons or cut pieces of paper, like second grade! It was boring. Once the music cycle ended, Miss Worth the artist, returned with a very different curriculum.

We found her in our homeroom math class seated at Mrs. Franke's desk, busy. She seemed to ignore us as we filed in, talking. While everyone took their seat, she silently drew lines. We finally all got very quiet, waiting for some kind of command. Nothing.

Finally, Chris said, "Miss Worth?"

"Oh, you're here. I was having so much fun. Come up and make a circle around this desk so you can see."

She had a large piece of white construction paper with a few pencil lines on it. In the center there were two parallel "Ss". On either side, was a straight line a few inches in from the end of the paper. Near the top was a curvy line running perpendicular to the straight lines along the sides. She had been pasting small irregularly cut pieces of blue construction paper at the top, above the curvy line.

"This," she said pointing to the blue, "Is the sky." Then, she started to paste pieces of irregularly cut brown pieces on the right hand side straight line. "This is a tree."

"What is this?" Asked Larissa.

"It's a collage."

"What's that?" asked Chucho.

"Bits of paper. Sometimes, artists stick all kinds of paper on paper like pieces of newsprint or even pictures but I'm doing a simple one."

"Are we going to do that?"

"We can if you want."

Soon, we were each seated at our desks with our own sheet of white paper and boxes of precut colored construction paper, a pencil and paste. "My suggestion is to look out the window and create a version of what you see," said Miss Worth.

While we all worked, she talked. "The Chinese invented paper over two thousand years ago. Legend has it that Chinese artists soon began to experiment with collages. A few hundred years later, the Japanese also experimented. During the last sixty years, Europeans and Americans have been playing with this idea. Some people mix paper and other objects. Some just paste paper. Next week, I can bring some slides of examples."

"Why did it takes us so long?" asked Eric.

"I don't know. What do you think?"

"The brown man is more creative," said Wuicho which set off a buzz of conversations.

"That's interesting," said Miss Worth. "Keep talking if you want but also keep pasting."

The class phonograph was open and set on a nearby table. As we talked and pasted, she breezily ambled over and put a record on the turn table, switched it on and placed the needle down. It was unusual piano music.

"What's that?" asked Roberta.

"It's Chopin," said Mert.

"Ah! Someone listens to the long hairs at home."

"Long hairs? Like the Beatles?"

"No, the original long hairs from hundreds of years ago who wrote and played music to amuse kings. Fédéric Chopin was a Polish composer and pianist. Most of his music is for the piano. This number is called Nocturne which is French for of the night."

"Hey! I'm Polish," said Craig.

"In Spanish, the word is *nocturno*," said Wuicho.

"Thank you."

"How come the words in French and Spanish are so similar?" asked Craig.

"They are romance languages, both based on Latin."

"Like they use in Mass."

"Correct. That's why it's called the Roman Catholic Church. Romans spoke Latin."

"If he's Polish why did he use a French name?" asked Chris.

"He lived in Paris for a long time."

"What did he die of?"

"He was sick most of his life. He died at thirty-nine of Tuberculosis."

"What's that?"

While this conversation continued, the music played. Students looked out the window, pasted, talked to friends. To anyone walking by the picture window, it must have looked out of control. Just before the bell rang, Miss Worth asked, "Should we continue this next week? Raise your hand if you think so."

Lots of hands went up. "Fine. Please write your name on the back and set them neatly in the box on the table. If you are satisfied with your art, you are welcome to start another next week. Look at magazine advertisements. You might see some very interesting pictures that give you ideas."

The strangest thing happened. Mr. Beard just disappeared. He had walked the hallways telling people not to bounce balls in the covered outside hallways because it echoed or interrogated students seated in the hallways. All of a sudden he didn't. One day, Mrs. Franke asked me to take her roll sheet to the office. While there, I snuck a look inside Mr. Beard's open office door. His family photos were all missing. The bookshelves empty, his paddle gone.

"Where's Mr. Beard?" I asked the secretary.

"You'll find out soon enough."

Without that hall monitor, almost every basketball player could be identified by the dribbling. We dribbled everywhere, all the time. Our Saturday morning practices became scrimmages. Now that the team was chosen we all showed up. Sometimes, others showed too, even older boys. So we began to vote on captains who chose teams. We had to take turns by substituting which usually was by agreement.

"Vic! Let me in for a while."

"*Dicho y hecho.*"

It became more difficult to figure out who was on your team when they changed so often. We decided to play shirts and skins. Skins were the boys who played with no shirt. This was problematic at the beginning since some boys were shy. Some for cosmetic reasons and others for darker reasons. For instance, Wuicho did not play skins for weeks. Vic finally confided, "When his father beats him, he uses a stick and it leaves welts on his back."

The first time he took off his t-shirt, there were long red marks all over his back but we just ignored them and played.

Our Saturday basketball no longer lasted an hour but often three hours. Boys came and went depending upon their schedules. Our skills improved rapidly.

Practice became very methodical. On offense we practiced changing our hands while dribbling, hoping that the defender might go off balance permitting us to dribble around him. We practiced the jumper, planting one foot so we could achieve a higher height. With the lay-up, we practiced dribbling to either side of the hoop. With shooting, we heard a lot less "bongs" and chain rumbles and more chimes. Most importantly, we were taught to move, pass and move again. On defense, we slid from side to side like in football to prevent our feet from crossing when we followed the ball. We kept our hands up in the air at all times to make a blocked shot or an intercepted pass more likely. When rebounding, coach showed us how to come down with the ball and cover it with two hands, moving our torso from side to side to prevent the opposing player from stealing it. We also learned how to play zone defense.

As we progressed, it was obvious that the best ball handlers were Vic, Chucho, Jim and Craig. The best rebounders were Eric, Cájame, Chris, Wuicho and Jed.

Shooting was different. The best inside shooters were Tacho and Eric. This started to define positions.

Coach believed that a strong defense won games. He taught us how to play a full court press and how to trap opposing players so that they made silly mistakes. The idea was to do everything possible and permissible to stop the opposing team from passing the half court line when they attempted to bring the ball in. Our mission was to force them to make a bad pass, intercept it and drive or pass and drive to the basket.

The night before our first game, Coach Esposti had a brown paper grocery bag full of game jerseys. He asked us to sit down on the court while he pulled one out. It was turquoise with a golden Thunderbird on the chest and a white number etched in gold on the back.

"Vic! What shirt size are you?"

"Size 18."

"That's about a men's small. Here." He handed Vic a jersey.

Vic opened it to read the number. "Fourteen! That's Bob Cousy's number!"

"You'll grow into it," deadpanned coach.

Our first game against Hohokam was at home. The janitor brought out an aluminum four tiered bleacher that he unfolded and set up on one sideline near midcourt. Like in football, teachers brought out students in a single file line. Once the bleachers were filled, they encircled the court. There was a scoring table set up opposite the bleachers with two chairs and cards with numbers on twin standup A-frames so the crowd would see the score. The score keepers flipped cards.

Many of basketball's rules have changed since then. For instance, we had no three point line. The game was tighter, near the basket. For eighth graders, a shot from the top of the key was difficult. Taking more than one step without dribbling was penalized more frequently. Likewise, more penalties were called on players who moved the ball from palm down to palm up while dribbling. This was called "palming the ball" while today it's called "carrying the ball." We played with a center, moving in and out of the key every three seconds. Officials do not tend to pay as much attention to this today. Coach Esposti shook hands with the other coach and they talked for a brief time, smiling. The officials were assigned by the district.

"Ready coach?'

"Right. Boys! Gather round. Starting lineup: Vic, Jim at guards, Wuicho and Jed at forwards and Eric at center. Hands in. Thunderbirds!"

We ran on court for the tip-off. They had a boy who must have been five feet ten inches tall and he tipped it to one of their guards. We immediately ran to their end of the court, took positions with our hands up. Vic waved his arms as well. He knew their guards from Little League and talked.

"Come on Bobby! Throw that ball."

Their guard Bobby took his eyes off of his moving teammates and Vic jabbed the ball out of his hands. Just like practice, it was off to the races. Vic dribbled, passed to Jim on his right who drove towards an empty hoop for a layup. It rolled around the rim and out into Eric's hands who put it in. Our shooting was so-so but we moved. At half time, we were ahead by three baskets. They never caught us.

After our Saturday morning basketball marathon, I pedaled north to my route for collections. Mrs. Hunsberger asked me to come in. Her dining room and kitchen areas were a mass of carboard boxes, stacked up four feet high. Her table had stacks of dirty dishes and glasses.

"I'll pay you one dollar extra if you could move some boxes for me," she said. She led me back into a bedroom also stacked high with cardboard boxes. "I want you to carry these ten boxes and stack them in the living room."

"Yes, ma'am."

On the way home, I pedaled down Eric's street. His dog was wandering the neighborhood. When it saw me, the dog began to charge. This time I had my squirt gun conveniently stuck in the back part of my pants. I pedaled just fast enough not to be a stationary target. When the dog reached my back tire, I fired lemonade right into his eyes.

Those Who Are Gone

That night, the same policeman I had seen in the hospital knocked on our front door. "Is your father home?"

When my dad came to the door, I took a step back and listened. "Bert, Wetzel has complained that your son Jack sprayed his dog with some sort of solution that caused it discomfort." My dad turned to me.

"Lemon juice and water. The dog was wandering the street and chased me."

"If the dog was loose, isn't that against the leash law?"

"Yes."

"I'd like to file a complaint." They sat down at the kitchen table.

At school, a man in a shirt and a tie walked the halls, warning us not to dribble in the halls. Later in the day, I saw him walking the halls again.

The next morning during our morning announcements on the intercom system, our principal concluded, "I'd like to welcome Mr. Dabrowski to our staff. He will be taking the Vice Principal position. Mr. Beard has been an officer in the army reserves for many years and his unit was activated. He is now serving in Indochina as Captain Beard. I know that all of you will keep him in your prayers."

At dinner that night, my dad said, "Dan will be leaving tomorrow morning. He will report for duty."

I looked over at Dan.

"I've been drafted."

"How long will you be gone?" I asked.

"Two years."

"What time do you have to leave?" I asked.

"Dad will drive me downtown. We have to be there by five in the morning. All inductees take an oath before an

87

eleven hour bus ride to Camp Roberts, north of Paso Robles in California."

"How long have you known this?" I asked.

"Ten days."

"Nobody tells me nothing." I said.

When I woke the next morning, I heard sobs.

I found my dad all alone seated at the kitchen table, weeping. I had never seen this in my life.

"Dad?"

He looked up, wiped his face with the palms of his hands and stood. "Come here, Jack." We embraced.

"You went to war..." I began.

"This war's different, son."

My mom came out and prepared coffee and some breakfast. Bacon popped. Smoke filled the air. As she cooked I asked, "What exactly do they teach army guys in training."

"How to kill," she responded and began to cry.

Halloween fell on a Saturday that year. After collections, I pedaled over to Vic's where he was outside setting up lights. His younger sister put objects on the outside rustic covered patio.

"Is this for trick or treaters?" I asked.

"We don't really celebrate Halloween. That's an Irish holiday. We celebrate the Day of the Dead on November first to honor our ancestors," he said as he climbed down a wooden ladder. "Come over here." He led me to the covered patio. "This is a photo of my grandfather, here's a photo of my great grandparents." He grabbed an old black bound journal and opened it. The pages were yellowed with age. "This is a list of my ancestors."

"So you don't give candy to children?"

"Tonight at midnight we will pray and read the names of the people in that book. Tomorrow we will picnic at my grandfather's grave in the Guadalupe Cemetery."

Eric showed up to school with a shaved head the day of our next game. I remembered my mother's comment that if she left the hair bleach on too long, her hair would fall out. Eric started to ignore Vic's breaks and Coach Esposti who already substituted liberally pulled him. "Cájame! Go get 'em." He became a rebounding machine. It got to the point that before he even touched ground with a rebound, Vic was loping down court. Cájame threw a lob and Vic followed with a lay-up. On offense it was beautiful. Miss? No problem. Cájame came down with it and immediately fed the closest guard for a mid-range jumper. Our shots were improving.

Unfortunately when coach put Eric back in, he wanted to prove something. Only a minute in, he jumped for a rebound and came down wrong. We all heard the loud crack and then saw him grimace, fall and scream. The game stopped. An ambulance drove down to courtside where two paramedics gently loaded him onto a stretcher and took him away.

We lost to Tonalea in a close game. Without Eric, our system wasn't the same.

That's when coach began to concentrate on plays. The first play was called Figure Eight. The coach held up eight fingers on the sideline and either guard shouted out "Eight." We immediately went into motion. If Jim or Craig were calling the play, we all ran clockwise because they were right handed. If Vic called the play, he also nodded to the right or left side since he played equally well with both hands. Generally speaking, we all went into motion. The center moved to forward, the other forward to center. While the play caller turned his back on his defender, the leading forward ran around him for a handoff. The play caller ran to the open forward position. The man with the ball was looking for a forward position moving towards the basket who might be wide open for a lay-up. If run quickly, it was very effective.

Another play had four of our five teammates form a line near to the baseline. While both forwards screened an opposing player, the guard darted out, then in towards the basket. We learned about basic ten plays, all signaled by the coach from the sideline with fingers held up, one through ten. Basically, we were no longer playing with a center but three forwards. It didn't bother Cájame.

One morning as I pedaled up to school, I noticed lots of tiny green toads hopping around at the bicycle racks. Once on campus I realized that the entire school grounds looked like a moving carpet. Who wants toad guts on their shoes? I put a foot out and brushed toads aside to make a space for a foot.

Tacho was also sweeping one foot from side to side. "Last night the elders told us that something important is on the horizon. We danced all night and the toads fell from the sky just before daybreak."

Most of the girls in the eighth grade screamed and ran to the girls bathroom, squishing them along the way and screaming more.

Even entering the classroom was crazy. The door opened and students ran in as toads followed, hopping, and girls screamed. Mrs. Franke did not scream.

"Craig, Wuicho, Chucho! Grab a waste can and start throwing toads into them."

Mert said, "In the Bible, God punished the Egyptians by raining frogs on them. It was called the Second Plague."

Once our room was clean, the boys just opened the door and tossed them out. But the toads did not disappear. A few minutes later, our principal came on the morning announcements to explain that we were the only school in the district affected by the plague. He said that it seemed to be related to the creek and told the teachers that our janitors would be handing out brooms before lunch so that appointed students could sweep paths to the cafeteria. Physical Education and basketball practice were canceled for the day.

After the announcements, class was again interrupted by a screaming girl who had a toad in her hair. Roberta reached over, picked it out and walked the toad to the door. She turned to the class and said, "Raining toads is a sign of good luck for the Yaquis. It means that rain and good fortune are coming."

We continued our day but each hour when the bell rang to change classrooms, screaming started all over again. Before the lunch bell, Mrs. Franke handed me a push broom.

"You will walk ahead of us. Use the broom to clear a path."

"Yes ma' am."

The next morning the toads were still there but less, much less. It was no longer a living carpet of hopping amphibians but just a few hopping around which was good since that night our first eighth grade dance was scheduled.

The school had brought back Miss Johnson, our music teacher, to train us in three dance steps: the two step, the box step and fast dancing. She showed us how to stand, where to put our hands and the basic steps. With the help of her metronome, we picked it up.

Girls were instructed to wear a dress that covered their knees. Boys were instructed to wear slacks and leather shoes. Jed and Chris rode their bicycles to my house. We all stopped at Jim's house and then pedaled to Yavapai.

The cafeteria was decorated with hand-painted posters. In front of the stage, there was a lunch table set up with a phonograph, records and a microphone for the disc jockey who was someone's older cousin. The table was flanked by speakers which faced a large semi-circle of chairs. In the back were several folding tables with refreshments supplied by the Parent/Teacher Association. They had lemonade and cookies. Coach Esposti, Mr. Dabrowski and Mrs. Franke chaperoned.

I had never seen our coach in a shirt and tie before. He looked a bit uncomfortable and tugged at the collar as he nodded. "Welcome, Colter."

The girls arrived in groups and took seats together, talking. The boys were less talkative. We all sat stoically as if marching to a death sentence.

"Did your mother practice with you?" I asked Jed.

"My older sister."

"What's she say?"

"She wouldn't dance with me in a million years. And she laughed!"

The disc jockey was like a radio personality, joking and playing records. Most of the jocks meandered over to the treats table until coach shooed us away. "Leave some for the girls. Get out there and dance."

Those Who Are Gone

So, we moved over to a section of chairs facing the girls who ignored us and talked. Roberta, Maritza and Ada must have walked because they all sat down in back and cleaned their shoes with napkins before taking a seat. Vic showed up late too.

"Where's Wuicho and the guys?"

"They didn't feel comfortable."

Jim said, "If someone doesn't dance with Larissa, we will have to deal with her mother." He straightened his tie and walked over, bowing to Larissa before taking her hand and leading her to the dance floor.

Jed grabbed his jaw and the side of his head and popped his neck. "Ready," he said and walked over to Mert.

Vic was next, dancing with Roberta. A few minutes later, Craig tapped him on the shoulder politely and took Roberta's hand.

I snuck back to the refreshment table where Coach Esposti slumped against a wall. "Colter!" He stood up straight.

"Dance with Elizabeth and I'll start you in our next game."

I looked over at Elizabeth, all alone, seated with her ankles crossed and hands folded on her legs. She was a very round girl whose thick glasses that always appeared crooked. "Yes, sir."

Eventually we took lemonade and cookies to the girls as instructed and tried to be nice. At eight twenty-five the light flickered and Mrs. Franke leaned over the disc jockey's shoulder to say into the microphone, "Last dance." She then put the phonograph needle on "Save the Last Dance for Me."

Coach walked behind us boys and said, "Man up! Make the girls smile."

The following week coach had Eric be his assistant, handing out towels and holding the clipboard. Eric's leg was broken in two places and had to be screwed together. His cast went from his crotch to his ankle which was much more difficult to navigate on crutches than mine. I did start the next game as a forward and Vic and Jim were kind enough to pass me the ball. It was Jed and Chris who were red hot that day, sinking shots inside and out. I especially liked seeing Jed do his post jump shot. He had this habit of quickly faking right and left before taking a step and going up. In this game, they were all looping high and going straight through, making the chains pop and clang. What a sound! We were rolling like a team.

Then, the sky got dark one afternoon while we were still in school. The wind began to howl so loud that we all got up to look out the window. Trees along the creek bent, swayed and the rain started to fall in giant pellets. Outside it smelled musty. This is an uncommon sight in the desert. The principal interrupted class to announce that weather authorities predicted worse in the coming hours and advised all teachers to let us go home early. That was the only day in my newspaper career that my mother drove me around my route.

By the time we got home, lawn chairs were flying through the air. Many people's bamboo slatted outside window coverings rolled and blew along the street. Roof shingles peeled off and flew away. Our metal public street light swayed as if it were made of licorice. Four inches of water ran down our street.

Both my mom and I were soaked just from running to get my bundle of papers earlier. My shoes squished with every step. Safe at home, we bathed and changed clothes. Dad came home and did the same before we all cooked some food. The rain had stopped when we turned the local news on the television, there was reporting about flooding along the wash. A reporter dressed in a long rain coat and hat which held on with one hand and pointed to a washed away section of McDowell Road with the other.

"Hey! That's right by Vic's house," I said.

My mom's brow wrinkled. "Try calling him."

"Hello? Jack! Yeah, we're all right but water is coming up through the floor. It popped all the wood knots out and everything is wet. The creek is still running. We're…"

The phone went dead. It was getting dark. My dad and I grabbed two flashlights before jumping into his car. The McDowell Road creek overcrossing was gone. There were road blocks, policemen and utility workers in orange suits. They had also set up temporary lights with gasoline powered generators. The road just wasn't there. In its place was a giant hole and a few feet lower, running water. My dad spoke to a policeman he knew and came back to the car.

"He said Yaqui Town electric power should be restored before daybreak but the phones will take longer. None of the homes collapsed but there's no way in or out right now. We can't do anything tonight, Jack."

Rain in the desert is strange. Although it might only last for minutes, there's always the chance of flooding since the ground is so hard and the creeks and streams are filled with dried plants and trees that often form dams. When those natural dams bust, it's a flash flood downstream, a wall of water.

The following morning when the bell, the covered halls echoed delighted chatter because all of our classmates were accounted for. As promised, electricity had been restored, the telephone was scheduled for repair that day and road crews were building a temporary crossing at McDowell and downstream at McKellips. Neighbors had brought small boats on trailers to be able to ferry people back and forth across the bloated creek. The entire area which we had been using for bicycle ramps was under water. Our basketball courts overlooked a river.

Over the next few days, the creek returned to normal and several local churches set up food drives, clothing drives and even building material drives to help repair the homes.

Yavapai and the newer homes were all built on a higher elevation and were not affected. We played our last game of the season at Pima School. Their school was also high and dry. Their team matched up well against us: about the same height and also very fast. Everybody on our team had minutes to play. Vic, Jed and Cájame scored most of our points but our defense ended the game for them. Vic, Craig and Jim all had steals which led to baskets. Jed and Chris both had blocks that resulted in lob passes downcourt to a streaking Jim or Craig. We played like a team, with lots of movement and timely passes.

Season over, classes ended on a Friday. The school district was having a longer Christmas break than normal that year. All I could think about was my older brother incommunicado on an army base. That night the phone rang just before dinner.

"Colter?"

"Yes."

"This is Coach Esposti. We have been invited to play in a Phoenix basketball tournament. Are you interested?"

"Yes."

"Bring one of your parents, jersey and playing clothes to the Yavapai cafeteria at eleven tomorrow morning. There is a permission slip to sign and I'll explain everything then. Our first game is tomorrow"

My parents did not even discuss it. They both said "Yes" simultaneously. The next morning, I was there with a gym bag at my side. Coach explained that this tournament was open statewide but he had just heard about it. The storm had wiped out several important highways across the state and many rural schools could not participate. For that reason, they were willing to let us play as a late admission. There were limits: players had to be five feet six inches or less in height and eighth graders.

"The fees are waived. I have some anonymous donors who will pay the entry fees and the cost of transportation. I already have scheduled two small vans to pick us up in an hour for our first game this afternoon."

There was a small folding table where my dad could fill out and sign the permission slip as a man measured my height. He read the wall mounted chart. Then, he looked down at my feet.

"Take your shoes off."
I did.
"Perfect! Right on the money. Next!"

We were only able to get eight players; Chris, Jed, Jim, Wuicho, Vic, Tacho, Chucho and me. Craig and Ricky had already left town for Christmas family gatherings.

Cájame was too tall. Even if Eric had been fit, he was also too tall.

All of the parents drove off and came back with brown bag lunches before we loaded up in the vans and were driven a few miles to East High on the Phoenix side of the Scottsdale/Phoenix border, near Hole in the Rock.

The parking lot was huge, the school sparkling new and modern with unusual colored concrete, decorative brick and exotic planters. Coach walked us to the enormous gym which was filled with people talking and bustling. There were a series of folding tables set up in a wide hall where coach lined us all up and started talking to an official.

"Right. We're a late entry with a game in thirty minutes…" He signed some papers and led us to a dressing room to throw on our playing clothes. While we slipped on jerseys and gym shoes, he talked. "We have two games set up for today. We'll play in a few minutes and then we'll have an hour break. We have played very well. Keep it up. I like what I see."

Walking into a real indoor gym was a bit like the sky opening. It was nearly filled with spectators from all over the state, holding homemade signs, blowing horns and whistles. The giant room with a ceiling sixty feet off the floor vibrated. Two teams were leaving the floor as we walked in and both had brand new zoomy, crisp uniforms. The players were of all colors and flavors.

Coach Esposti led us to a bench. "Vic! Run the team through our normal warm-ups. Boys! This court is the same size as Yavapai's and the rules are also the same. I'll be right back. I have to turn in some papers." On the other side of the court there were two folding tables set up with four men talking, shuffling papers and adjusting a microphone. Coach handed them some sheets of paper and listened to them while

Vic had us start some basic calisthenics. Off to one side, two officials in zebra striped shirts stood with arms crossed, chatting.

We had never played a game where everyone was about the same size. It seemed strange to see Chris enter the midcourt circle. "Movement!" yelled Coach Esposti just before tipoff.

"Look at those cheesy jerseys," an opposing player said to a teammate.

"Hey! You sure they're from this side of the border?"

"Ready?" the official asked Chris, then repeated the question for the opposing player. The ball went up. Chris tipped it to Vic who immediately called out "Eight!"

We ran and didn't stop. Within seconds, Jed was wide open and made a layup. Without a word, we ran to the opposite side of the court and got those hands up in the air like butterflies spreading their wings. Jim managed to steal the ball from their point guard. Vic was already sprinting down the side of the court, received the pass and dribbled in for a layup. Coach sat on our bench, expressionless.

It continued like this throughout the game. Although the other players were dressed like a professional team, they couldn't keep up with us. All of those long bicycle trips and Saturday basketball marathons had worked magic. They had a full roster of twelve and their coach substituted every three or four minutes. Coach Esposti waited until we were fourteen points ahead in the fourth quarter before he sent Chucho, Tacho and me in.

"Here come the scrubs," said an opposing player.

"Which rez are you guys from?" asked another as we silently took our places. We had the ball and brought it in. Jed passed to Tacho who passed to me near the key. I took a mid-range jumper which arced high and fell straight through without a sound because these hoops had cloth instead of chain nets. I looked over at the haters and just smiled.

We shook hands before filing out to the hall where coach offered to buy us soft drinks from a machine. "Some sugar in your system might be a good idea." Then, he led us outside to an alcove with concrete benches where we quickly ate our brown bag lunches.

Coach checked his wrist watch and asked, "Do you want to watch a bit of the game before ours?"

Back in the gym, it was the final four minutes of the fourth quarter with Hohokam behind by five baskets, a lot for eighth graders. They seemed dejected and tired. At the buzzer, they all trudged towards their bench.

Within minutes, we took the court for warmups. The Hohokam team coach motioned to Coach Esposti who limped over. They turned their back to us as they spoke. Our coach nodded and shook hands before trudging towards us as we began our passing drill. Coach just watched with his hands on his hips. Vic led us into layup drills. An official lightly blew his whistle and Coach Esposti motioned for us to form a circle.

"The opposition may taunt you. Ignore them and play ball. No pushing, shoving or hitting." He looked at Vic. "Try passing to your right, not left." Vic nodded. "This team likes to talk. Just let 'em waste their breath."

They won the tipoff, passing to a point guard who did not hesitate: he dribbled full speed down court. However, at the top of the key Jed and Chris came from either angle and trapped him. Chris jumped with his arms moving like a windmill while Jed was poking. Their player made a frantic bounce pass which was intercepted by Jim who passed to a racing Vic who then passed to a streaking Jed. Basket!

Those Who Are Gone

On their next in-bounds, they made better passes and a great jumper to tie the score. The game went back and forth throughout the first half with us leading by two baskets at half time. In the second half, the officials began to call more fouls. I noticed that the opposition players were knocking shoulders with our players as they all lined up on the key. It was difficult to hear, but we could see mouths moving.

Halfway through the third quarter, we were still ahead by two baskets but Vic had three fouls. Coach pulled him and put me in. For the first time, I heard the other players clearly. They were talking down and dirty. Although we had been warned, our team was frustrated and making silly mistakes.

I played until the end of the quarter without much of a contribution so coach put Chucho in my place. He and Wuicho started connecting. More importantly, they were passing well on the set plays. The score went back and forth.

Vic reentered the game at the beginning of the fourth quarter but fouled out in minutes. When he walked to the bench, coach asked him, "What exactly was that player telling you?"

"He said things about my sister."
"Do you know this guy?"
"No."
"How could he possibly know your sister? He lives in Tucson. This is a Tucson team, Vic."
They won by two baskets. As we filed past them to shake hands we heard:
"Injun chumps."

"Losers."

We all slunk off the court and walked towards the vans. While walking, coach said, "We have a game tomorrow at ten in the morning so I will need you boys at Yavapai by nine. Make sure you wash those jerseys!" Coach held his nose and grimaced.

"But we lost," said Chris.

"This tournament is a double elimination," answered coach. "From now on we play to win. If we lose one more game, we're out. Please have your parents prepare a sack lunch and tell them you may not be home until four in the afternoon. We will drop you off." Coach motioned to me. "Colter! I need to talk to you." He moved off to one side with his back to the team and whispered, "Don't lose more weight."

My brother had written to us. He explained in the letter that his day started before the sun rose and did not end until late at night. He said that they were busier than he had ever been before but well fed. He also gave us an address if we wanted to write to him and explained that he would be there until the middle of January.

"He would like us to write," said my mom.

"Mail call is a big thing when you're in the armed forces," said my dad.

The next morning, we arrived just in time for warmups. Everyone seemed to run them faster than normal. As we all took our places for the tip-off, Jed cracked his neck. Jim intertwined his finger and pushed them palms out with a sort of rolling cracking noise. Vic's rolled his shoulders. Chris slapped his hands together, bent his knees slightly and bent at the waist. The ball went up and Chris tapped it right to Jim who passed to a running Vic down a sideline who passed it to Jed running down the middle. Basket.

I have no idea what anyone ate the night before but it was as if we were all super-charged. The thirty-two minute game seemed like a half minute. As coach insisted, we ignored everything said to us except for the whistles and commands by game officials. In the third quarter, we ran three of our set plays which worked well. Coach stood in front of the bench with his hands locked behind his back.

By the last four minutes of the fourth quarter, when Jed sunk one of corner jumpers. Coach Esposti called a time out.

"Let's have some fun. Full court press." He looked up and pointed to the scoreboard. We're four points ahead, Open it up. Thunderbirds on three. One, two… "

"Thunderbirds.!"

We went into action and sure enough, intimidated them into passing poorly. Chris made a layup. We immediately went into the press again. The player trying to pass the ball in had a startled face like his dog just got run over by the garbage truck. Bad pass. Another basket. We gave them another look but as their man confidently slapped the ball, we ran into a third press. Chris intercepted their pass at midcourt and threw a fastball type pass to Jed in that corner who went up. A sixth point.

They fell apart. We won by fourteen points. Coach suggested that we eat lunch early and led us to a quiet alcove with large plants, nice concrete benches and seats. After that win, we were very talkative.

The noon game was not even close. Coach moved us in and out, substituting. Everyone on the team scored something and we coasted to victory. After, coach bought us all soda pops and one of the drivers opened a large cardboard box of chocolate covered cake donuts.

Even after the third game warmups, Wuicho, Tacho and I all were foot-tapping on the sidelines. As we made a circle for last minute instruction, coach handed out chewing gum. "Studies show that those who chew gum get higher scores on tests. Here's a paper wrapper. Stick it into the top of your sock for when you want to ditch the gum. Do not spit it on the court. Use the wrapper and return it to the top of your sock."

In this game, coach called a lot of preset plays, usually standing with his fingers held high. We used all ten and even used the Figure Eight three times. They were all effective, so effective that we did not use a full court press. Again, we all played and just about everyone scored something.

We won but by the last whistle our shoulders slumped, some of us shuffled our feet as we shook hands with the opposing team.

"Rest. Our next game is Saturday at noon. This will be a semifinal game. The winners will play on Sunday at noon. Tell your parents in case they can make it. If they can't, we'll bring you home. Oh! How 'bout we practice on Tuesday and Thursday at two in the afternoon? I'd like to go over some basics."

At dinner, I slumped a bit in my chair as my dad asked about our games. "We're moving on to the semi-finals next Saturday."

"How do you feel?" he asked.

"Tired and sore."

"Take a hot bath," suggested my mom.

On Monday, I slept in. Vic called. "Let's shoot before delivering papers."

Those Who Are Gone

"What time?"

"One."

The entire team was there. First we sat down and just talked about the games, our strengths and weaknesses. We decided to have a shoot around for no more than one hour. Since several of us had balls, we divided into four groups of two. A pair of us each went to a hoop and took turns. One guy fed the other for twenty shots, then we switched. We mixed the pairs up and continued and mixed again. Then, we practiced layups with one player leading the other so if he missed it, the trailer was supposed to grab the rebound and toss it in.

Vic and I rode off to pick up our papers. The weekend games had set me back on collections, so for those customers who I knew were retired or worked an early shift, I started knocking. As I was finishing my route, I noticed a police car and the dog catcher's truck in front of Eric's house.

Four hours later as we ate dinner, the same policeman who had helped us in the hospital and had stopped by once knocked on the front door.

"Bert, Wetzel's dog is dead," said the officer.

"What happened?"

"This afternoon someone must have been taunting him from the alley. The dog was chained in Wetzel's yard with a choke collar. The dog became so incensed that he ran and jumped the fence, attempting to attack the person, hanging itself. I thought you and Jack should know."

"Want a cup of coffee?"

"Nah. I've got to return to duty. Next time."

On Tuesday, coach Esposti had us run for eight minutes around the school yard before we lined up in two facing lines along the painted key. Coach pointed to one side. "You are the offense." He pointed to the other side. "You are the defense. We are going to practice footwork about boxing the offensive player out when going for a rebound." Coach lightly touched Jim's shoulders. "Jim's offense. He's going to move to his right to grab a rebound. The defense doesn't want him to have position. Okay Jim. Move slowly to your right." As he moved, coach said, "Chris is the defense. To stop him, Chris is going to move to his left, turn his back and get those hands up for the rebound. It is also a good idea to stick your butt out. Nobody calls a foul on your butt."

We all laughed. "Let's try it slow first," said coach. "Pretend you're in a slow motion movie." As we practiced, we went faster and faster until we were at normal speed.

Coach blew his whistle. "Line up here, two lines single file." He pointed to each side of the lane. "I'm going to yell 'Go!' and toss the ball up at the rim. Right is offense. left is defense. Box him out and get the rebound if you can."

Coach stood off to his left side, yelled and tossed the ball up at the rim. It clanked and bounced as we battled for position. Sometimes nobody could grab it.

"If you listen closely while you're moving, the ball will sound different as it hits different sides of the rim." While we watched, he walked to the other side of the key and tossed it up at the rim. It clanked but had a slightly different sound. Likewise, the sound was a bit different when he threw it from the free throw. He stationed us at eight points on an arch around the hoop. "Listen and catch." He started throwing the ball up at the hoop from the same three

Those Who Are Gone

points and we just listened and grabbed the ball if it came in our direction.

The next day, the team brought more balls. We held our own shoot around but this time more informal. After about forty minutes, we ran around the school yard for eight minutes and then did wind sprints on the football field. I beat several players.

Thursday, we reviewed rebounding footwork. Then, coach divided us into two groups of four and told us to play. He watched. When he saw something he did not like, he blew his whistle and explained. Last, we practiced how and when to poke for the ball. "It's all about timing. You don't want to foul," explained Coach Esposti. Last, he told us, "If you are defending against a man with the ball and he is paying more attention to his players or the defenders — in other words, he is not paying attention to you — grab the ball right out of his hands and go, baby."

Coach lined us up single file. He held the ball and pretended to look downcourt, foolishly holding the ball exposed. We practiced ripping it out of his hands and starting to dribble downcourt.

Meeting on Saturday at eleven was much easier.

The gym was not as filled as the weekend before since only four teams would play two games. We were the first. Chris's mom and dad were in the stands. Jim's parents were there. Mrs. Franke and her adult son were there along with Miss Johnson.

We had not played this team before. They warmed up without a word and did not even glance at us. After some calisthenics, coach had us just shoot around.

They were a very disciplined team, running preset plays, moving in unison following the ball and not talking. There was no garbage talk at all. It was actually a bit different because they didn't even talk to each other much whether they made a mistake or did something well. Their coach screamed, often. He berated them for this or that and they played like robots.

They had quite the crowd in the stands, holding very fancy signs but they also did not rain down insults or blow loud horns. They clapped and yelled.

It was a close game at half time. We were ahead by a basket. During the break, coach took us to the snack room and gave us each a lollypop to suck on while he talked. "Let's use those boxing-out skills more in the second half on both sides of the court. On our side, look for that second or even third shot, especially near the hoop. On their side, look down court for anyone on our team streaking."

During the third quarter, Chris went up for a layup and an opposing player leaned into him with a shoulder. His legs went out from under him and he slammed down on the wooden floor. Jim helped him up and Chris kind of bent over. Coach called a timeout.

"Are you all right?"

"It hurts to breathe."

Coach looked up into the stands and waved to Chris's father before consulting with an on-court official and then the men at the scoring table. Chris's parents walked him off the court. We were now playing with seven.

"Wuicho. You're in. That boy might just have made a bad move. Do not punish anyone, just play ball."

The rest of the team was angry. All of a sudden, there were more steals and the rebounding was incredible with lots of butt work which the other coach screamed about. The officials ignored him. Coach Esposti stood silently.

We won and the other team members were very polite while their coach sneered. Instead of shaking our hands, he just kind of slapped at them.

One of the men from the scoring table told Coach Esposti, "He'll never be invited back."

Coach nodded.

Jim's parents volunteered to take Jed, Vic, and Tacho home which meant that we had an empty van. The volunteer driver loaded the rest of us up as coach waved. He decided to stay to scout the next game. "See you on Tuesday. Same place. Same time," he shouted.

We got in touch with Chris by phone later that day. The x-rays denoted a cracked rib and he would be bandaged up for a few days. "The doctor said I might be able to play next Saturday depending on how I feel."

Vic told him to report to Romualda, Monday at ten in the morning. Chris's mom said that she would drive him over.

We had our own private practice on Monday, repeating everything like the week before. At one point, Wuicho and I played guards. He made a great shot and I ran over to slap his back. He winched and I realized that he must have had welts again.

"When I turn eighteen, I'm out of here. I'll enlist," he confided.

Vic reported on Chris since he had translated earlier in the morning. He said that Romualda helped him unwrap the elastic bandage. She inspected the purple area, according to Vic, and touched it lightly. She bowed her head and held her finger on the spot for several seconds before smiling and rewrapping with a poultice.

"My grandmother says that he will be fine," reported Vic. "He needs to drink a special tea."

At Tuesday's practice, coach told us that the mouthy team that had beat us would be our opponent. He said that the key to beating them would be defense. We practiced steals, rebounding, and boxing out.

Jed had an older brother who played on the high school varsity football team as a lineman. He looked like a bear with a full black beard, scary. When we met on Wednesday for our coach-less practice, Jed handed out thin strips of paper with a funny saying on each.

"My brother says that the best ammunition for garbage talk is a funny rebuttal. He typed these up for us to memorize."

Mine said, "If I had a face like yours, I'd sue my parents." Vic's said, "Do you kiss your mother with that mouth?" Jim's was, "You sound better with your mouth closed." They were all good.

At home, my mom helped me respond to my brother. At the hardware store she bought a light bulb, a two foot long two by four and a light bulb receptacle with a plug. We drove to a sign shop where she asked the manager if they had a remnants box. He led us to a large bin full of pieces of plastic. She grabbed a piece of clear plastic and asked if they could cut it to eleven inches by seventeen.

"Sure."

Back at home, she screwed the bulb into the receptacle and placed it on our kitchen table. She set the two by four on edge a few inches above the light, then placed the plastic on top. She plugged it in, flipped the switch and said.

"*Voila*! A light table. Now you can trace our family tree for your brother."

The gym was raucous. There were signs, horns and people dressed in casual clothes as well as costumes. On our side were most of the eighth grade teachers, many waving turquoise and gold streamers. Some of our parents were there too. Coach asked Vic to lead us in calisthenics. Afterwards, we went into our layup drill. As I made mine and turned to grab the rebound and pass it out, I noticed the other team glaring and mouthing horrible things, then laughing.

The officials watched the game more closely than the previous ones. Within two minutes they called a foul on the opposing team. As we lined up along the key, I saw a member of the other team say something to Tacho who put his head down and said something back. The other player pushed him and whistles blew. It was a technical foul. The player's number was reported and noted.

Tacho had taken Chris's place and was doing very well. Chris had shown us his rib cage. The deep purple bruise had now become yellowish and he said he could breathe okay but coach asked him to sit out the first quarter. We ran three of our set plays and scored on all of them. We out rebounded them. On defense, rebounding accounted for quite a few of our points.

At the break between first and second quarters, coach told Chris, "Go get 'em." And Chris pulled off a sweatshirt he had been wearing over his jersey.

He didn't look rusty at all. He looked like a madman, rebounding and throwing elbows as he came down. Once he caught an opposing player right on the cheek. The player fell down and the whistles blew. As the team lined up along the key more words were exchanged and the shooter took a swing at Chris who clenched him like a boxer. Whistles blew. They let the player take his shot and then, he was ejected. Officials escorted him out of the gym as he yelled obscenities.

Coach pulled Chris and rotated positions sending Wuicho in. This was our small line-up. They started taking shots from the outside. Rebounds dropped and the score went back and forth.

Chris returned in the second half. Jim was hot, driving in and from the outside. Then Jed lit them up with his corner shots. The other team seemed to talk even more and each time, our team responded. By the fourth quarter with two minutes left, the other team had lost three players because of fights. Our starting five looked like they had just taken a shower, fully clothed. The other team now had nine to our eight but were ahead by six points. Coach stood, wringing his hands behind his back.

Wuicho nudged me and pointed. Vic's father and mother walked in the gym and began to climb the bleachers for a seat behind the team. Coach called a time out.

The team formed a circle around coach on the sidelines as I handed out white towels. Wuicho whispered to Vic as coach asked, "Anybody want to come out?"

Chris was the first to respond. "I came to win a championship."

"Me too."

"Me too,"

Jim nodded as did Jed.

Vic stared up at the bleachers. His jaw set and the muscles on his neck tensed.

"Vic?' asked coach.

"Let's cream them," he said.

"Press, men," said coach. "And don't stop pressing."

Those Who Are Gone

It was their ball to bring in under the basket. Vic jumped and waved his arms and talked. There was a nice bounce pass by the sideline where our team trapped and in desperation, their player threw a wild, looping pass that Jed intercepted and popped a mid-range jumper. It sank.

Chucho, Tacho and I all jumped up together, screaming.

"*¡Eso!*"

"*¡Eh la moey!*"

"*¡Dale!*"

Coach stood next to us. He glanced over and for a split second, smiled.

We pressed again. This time Vic caught a finger on the ball and it deflected to Jed who passed it back to Vic almost under the basket. He sent up an underhanded ball with spin that bounced on the backboard lightly and rolled around and through the net. We pressed a third time. They passed to a man at midcourt who foolishly tried to waste time by dribbling. As Chris met him with arms flaying, Vic swooped in from behind and managed to poke the ball up in the air. Somehow Vic retrieved it and raced for a layup.

Coach Esposti screamed, "*¡Orale macho! Nuestro pequeño Cousey.*"

Wuicho looked at me, surprised. We were both surprised.

The opposing coach called a timeout. They came back to the court and formed a single line facing their man with the ball. He slapped the ball and they moved. The inbounder managed to pass it to someone twenty feet away. Before we could trap, he passed to someone at midcourt who was covered by Chris with our entire team running. As he turned to pass, Vic ripped the ball out of his hands and started the streak. The clock was clicking down. Vic passed to Jed on the sideline and kept streaking. Jed passed it back to him just like in practice and he leaped up so gracefully. The ball bounced off the backboard and rolled through the net. The wooden floor vibrated as the crowd screamed.

With seconds left, they managed to pass it in to someone near our basket. He turned and threw an air ball in a last ditch effort to tie the score. It missed the rim as the buzzer sounded.

I didn't see or hear anything as we all ran onto the court, coach limping behind. While we were celebrating, a photographer tried to line us all up for a photo. Vic was looking in his parent's direction. "Anyone with parents here is welcome to greet them before the photo," said coach.

"Wait! This is for the Phoenix Republic."

"You can wait," said Coach Esposti.

Vic jogged over in front of his parents and meekly waved. His father stood, clapping and nodded.

Maybe my role was always meant to be as a witness. To this day, every member of our Thunderbird team still has a yellowed, cut out copy of that newspaper photo even though none of us live in South Scottsdale anymore. We've all become Hohokam, those who are gone.

Those Who Are Gone

Lawrence F. Lihosit

Lawrence F. Lihosit was born in the southern suburbs of Chicago, Illinois in 1951. His family later moved to Arizona where he graduated from Yavapai Elementary School, Coronado High School and Arizona State University. He reluctantly served in the U.S. Army Reserves during the closing years of the Vietnam War and enthusiastically volunteered for the Peace Corps (Honduras, 1975-1977).

Those Who Are Gone

OTHER BOOKS BY THE AUTHOR

South of the Frontera; A Peace Corps Memoir

Peace Corps Bibliography

Peace Corps Chronology; 1961-2010

Peace Corps Experience: Write and Publish Your Memoir

Slacker's Confession: Essays and Sketches

Madera Sketchbook

*Neighbors: Oral History from Madera, California
(Volumes 1, 2 & 3)*

Back to School and Other Poems

Border Penance and Other Stories

Americruise

*Jesus Was Arrested in Mexico City
and Missed the Wedding*

Travels in South America

Across the Yucatan

Years On and Other Travel Essays

Sound Machine: Flat-Top Guitars-Material & Care

Lawrence F. Lihosit

Printed in Great Britain
by Amazon